Burn Me Up Fast

BT Rockwell

ISBN 978-0692308172

Editors: Megan Fox and Paul Weisser, Ph.D.

Cover art: Josh Vanover

Book Layout: Eli Morgan

Special thanks to:

(The *real*) Megan Fox for making this possible. I undoubtedly needed your help from beginning to end.

Also thanks to:
Shirley and Dan for their unconditional love and support. Joel and Anne for consistently exposing me to knowledge and culture. The Doc, aka Lex Beats, for first showing me — well, everything. Sensei Konner for lessons in Eastern philosophy and always seeing a silver lining. Monica and Amy for being my saviors of sanity. Ph.D. Paul for his professional wisdom. Anna Patrick for wanting to be my expert publicist. Josh Vanover and Jared Liner for the perfect cover art. Davin Black for the incredible trailer. Mitch for providing me with a great place to write. Shallah Raekwon for letting me in on something supremely special. Dr. Hunter S. Thompson for unknowingly assisting me in establishing a point of view. Schenectady Scottie for experiencing the road with me like Cassady and Kerouac. All the entrusted friends and family who gave great suggestions for this story. Everyone who has ever believed in me on this (long) strange trip…

For Pumpkin Spice

There is no greater pleasure than seeing your loved ones prosper.

—The Fortune Cookie

1

"Ah, putain. Renée, ce express est degueulasse."

"Oh, stop, Jean," pleaded the woman on the other side of the table in a gentle French accent. "The espresso isn't disgusting. We've been in the States for less than a week, and already you're getting on my nerves."

Jean sipped from a small cup and looked at the few other tables set up outside the French café.

"Donc, c'est ca un café français à New York, hein?" he remarked, still sounding unimpressed.

Looking up at the striped umbrella blocking the strong July sun, Renée pulled out a slender cigarette as she sipped her iced coffee.

"I think this café has charm. This whole neighborhood does." She pointed to the laminated map on the table in front of her.

"Ecouté, as I have been trying to tell you, to get to Broadway we have to go south to Houston and then make a right until we reach Broadway. Simple, *oui?"*

"Oui."

Across the street, a boy wearing a black fitted Yankees cap and black T-shirt whistled as he rode his silver Mongoose. First, he headed north up Avenue A, but then he turned around and rode back the other way, whistling and jumping over curbs.

"Goat cheese and spinach quiche with a green salad," the

waitress said, handing the couple their matching plates. She passed the couple a bottle of vinaigrette and went back inside.

Renée folded up her map and slid it into her purse, which was hanging off her chair.

When the light changed to green, the boy on his bike crossed to the other side of the avenue, jumped onto the sidewalk with ease, and began to pick up speed toward the café. A few people dodged out of the way as he swerved forward through the pedestrians who were starting to make their way home from work.

"Looks delicious, no?" Renée said as she glanced down at her plate.

"*Ca manque de poivre*," replied Jean, turning to a busboy who was busy filling glasses of water. "*Excusez moi*. But can I please get some black pepper?"

With one perfect swoop, the boy in the Yankees cap grabbed the French woman's large purse and bolted around the corner, pedaling as fast as his legs would go, with the purse strap tightly wound around his left hand.

He made it two long blocks east to Avenue C when a voice called out, "Yo, Ajani! Ajani! Yo, I'm right here!"

Ajani saw Pedro, his accomplice, waving him down. He squeezed on his brake so hard that he almost flew over the handlebars as his front tire skidded to a stop.

"Hey, what's up?" Ajani said as he pulled his bike off the street and onto the sidewalk.

Pedro was waiting with a plastic shopping bag. Ajani threw the purse and his hat into it, and quickly took off his black shirt, revealing a wifebeater underneath. "We good?" he asked.

"Yeah," said Pedro as he wiped his forehead. His weight caused him to sweat profusely. "Hurry. Get the fuck outta here, yo."

"I'll see you at the Mound in a bit. Don't be late." Ajani jetted off on his Mongoose, heading east.

"Don't worry about me, nigga. I'll be there."

Pedro wiped his forehead again, flicked off the sweat, and headed on foot in the opposite direction.

2

THE ISLAND OF DOUBT —IT'S LIKE THE TASTE OF
MEDICINE.

—DAVID BYRNE
"CROSSEYED AND PAINLESS"

I'M A PIECE OF SHIT. I FEEL SOMETHING DEEP
DOWN. A PAIN. A SADNESS. ANXIETY. RESENTMENT
DIRECTED RIGHT AT LIFE ITSELF. A FEAR. A DOUBT.
THIS WORLD IS FUCKED AND SO AM I. MAYBE
IT'S NOT ALL THAT BAD AND MAYBE IT IS. BUT
WHICHEVER WAY IT IS, THIS GAME IS A CROOKED
ONE WITH SHIFTY MOTIVES AND SLIPPERY SLEIGHTS
OF HAND. I KNOW I'M NOT THE FIRST TO FEEL
THAT CONSTANT STRUGGLE. THAT OVERBEARING
BURDEN WEIGHING DOWN ON THE SHOULDERS HAS
BROKEN MORE THAN ONE STURDY BACK. AS FOR
ME, WELL, LET'S JUST SAY I'M PRETTY MUCH AT
THE BREAKING POINT.

"Yo, Byron! Put that shit down already!" Primo called. "Stop
writin' for a minute and join us on planet Earth, aight?"
I put my journal in my back pocket and took a long look at

the red and green dragon that Primo was getting tattooed on his shoulder. He winced in pain but just slightly. The tattoo parlor we were sitting in was clean and lofty. Giant pieces of Japanese artwork hung from all the walls.

"Craig, that's lookin' pretty damn official," I said.

"After ten years of scarring people, I better be good at what I do, B. Practice, practice, practice. Hell, I just feel bad for the first few dozen that I had to practice on." He said this with a smirk.

"It looks like you practiced on yourself," Primo said. "How many tats *you* have?"

"Lost count at thirty," Craig answered. His big Irish body was covered from ankle to Adam's apple. "I think we're all finished here."

"Sick," Primo said, gazing at the menacing dragon in the mirror. Then he pulled out a vacuum-sealed bag from his pocket. "Here. This is for you. It's Skywalker OG Kush."

"Ha," said Craig. "I didn't know Luke grew the green."

"He don't," Primo said. "But Leia does."

We all laughed.

"I'm not gonna open it now," said Craig as he threw the bag in a drawer. "If it's from you two, I'm sure it's off the hook."

"Is that enough for the dragon?" Primo asked.

"Sure," Craig said. "Just send me some of that business you got, too. Cool? You don't know how bad this helps right now. Life's fuckin' stressful these days."

"I know. For all of us. Fuckin' recession won't quit," Primo bitched, pulling out a blunt. "How about we smoke this up? Craig, you're about due for a break, right?"

"Yeah, let's do it."

The three of us walked outside in east Chinatown and around the corner, deep into an alleyway. The tall rundown buildings shaded us from the blazing sun. Primo lit up the blunt, taking a few huge drags, then passed it over to Craig.

A siren blurted! Red and blue lights reflected off the aged brick apartment building in the alleyway, lighting it up like a Christmas tree. One after the other, Primo and I jumped up on a green garbage dumpster and hopped over a chainlink fence. I barely made it to the ground without breaking my left ankle. Craig was last. He threw down the blunt and followed but was too big to nimbly climb over the fence.

"Freeze! Don't fucking move a finger, you piece of shit!" shouted one of the officers as he pointed his pistol.

Within seconds, they had Craig with his hands interlocked behind his head. The dumpster next to me stank like rotten fish. I could hear something rustling around in there, scrounging for food.

It was time to keep it moving. Primo and I sprinted all the way to my place on the corner of 6th Street and Avenue C.

When I opened the door to my apartment, I instantly got a whiff of weed still lingering in the air. That was pretty much how it always was. I pulled my journal out from my back pocket and dropped it on the desk next to my MacBook Pro.

"They got Craig." I was still catching my breath.

"Fuck," Primo said. "I don't think he's got any warrants, so he'll be out by tonight. Sucks though. Just for smokin' a blunt. What the hell? Did they get a look at us, ya think?"

"Nah, I don't think so."

"Well, I gotta light somethin' up after that," he said.

"Definitely."

Primo rummaged through some jars of pot I had on my desk as I gutted a Dutch in the garbage can.

"Yo, I'm sick of that OG for now," he said. "We burned so much of it. Let's smoke some of this." He opened one of the jars.

"Which is that? The Chem Guava or the Star Dawg?"

"The Star. It's so damn resinous. Shit. Smells like tangerines."

Primo and I have rolled together since we were kids. In fact, you could say we've pretty much known each other since birth. Norah, my mother, was and still is a nurse at Gouverneur Hospital. About six months after I was born, she helped the doctor give birth to Michael Hernández — or, as everyone called him, Primo. It wasn't long before we had scheduled play dates.

I finished rolling the blunt and lit it.

"Yo, B, after we finish this, let's book outta here," Primo said. "I got some errands to run. I want you to come with, aight?"

"I can't. I gotta go see Norah for dinner. I promised her."

"Yo, your mom can wait. We got shit to do right now."

I sighed.

"Just come with me. It's all good, aight? Just break me off a quarter pound of that Cali Kush for this woman first. Then we need to bounce."

What can I say? I went along. The man had a way with me. It was in my best interest anyway. Business is business.

3

Ajani met his good friend Chris Parker about ten blocks away from where he had lifted the purse. The two rode on the pathway over the FDR Expressway. Once they crossed the highway, they took the ramp down into the park nestled along the East River. The boys rode north beside the water on a newly laid promenade. Ajani led the way, speeding as fast as he could, with Chris Parker trailing closely behind him. They popped wheelies and jumped on and off the curbs that separated the cement from the manicured grass and shrubs.

Jumping off their bikes, the boys stashed them between a fence at the end of the promenade and the tall bushes that covered it. Then they squeezed through a hole they had cut out in the fence over a year earlier. A mound of large stones was the only thing that separated Ajani and his friend from the river. A few of the stones had smooth, flat tops, creating perfect seats.

The Mound was quiet and private. It was the perfect getaway from the organized chaos of the Lower East Side. Ajani and his friends sat there often, chugging Mountain Dew while scoffing down 50-cent chips.

Wispy pink clouds stretched across the light blue sky. A crescent moon already hung brightly over the low Brooklyn skyline. To the north stood the Queensboro Bridge. To the south was the

Williamsburg Bridge leading to Brooklyn.

Ajani watched as planes flew overhead from different directions. This was not coincidental. He had, in fact, carefully picked the location. The Mound was closely centered in the triangle of New York's and New Jersey's major airports.

The two boys waited patiently, cracking jokes and gossiping about classmates. Almost an hour later, the bushes near the fence started to rustle. Ajani looked up cautiously.

"What up, yo?" Pedro said from the other side of the fence. He forced his extra-wide body through the hole. "I told you two, yo. We gotta cut this hole bigger. Y'all are skinny fucks." He reached back through the hole and grabbed the white shopping bag with the purse in it. "Let's do this," he said, throwing the purse onto one of the large, flat stones.

The three kneeled down around the purse as Ajani rummaged inside. First, he grabbed the wallet. "You better not have combed through this already, Pedro."

"Yeah," agreed Chris Parker.

"Man, fuck you two!" Pedro said. "I didn't go through nothin'. And if I did, you wouldn't know anyway. So fuck you!"

"You better not have," Chris Parker said. "Or Ajani's gonna Atomic Wedgie your ass."

"Whatever, yo. I ain't scared of you two niggas. Just open the wallet."

Ajani went through the tan and taupe wallet. "Three hundred and seven dollars. Sweet. That's over a hundred bucks for each of us. There's credit cards, but we shouldn't be holdin' on to that shit anyway."

"So throw the rest in the river," Chris Parker said.

"But save the wallet," Pedro cut in. "I wanna give it to my *abuela*."

"What if she asks how you got it?" Ajani asked.

"I'll say I found it in your mama's closet, yo. She won't give a fuck. Trust me."

Ajani gave the wallet to Pedro and threw the purse into the East

River. The murky waters instantly swallowed it up.

"I found another spot we can try tomorrow maybe," Chris Parker said. "It's on Ludlow."

"Good." Ajani divvied up the money. "But tomorrow's too soon. Let's think of somethin' else for tomorrow."

"I'm sick of these bullshit schemes, yo," said Pedro. "Did you talk to Byron yet about that blow?"

"Nah, man. Why you keep harassin' me about that shit?" Ajani skipped a pebble off the surface of the river.

"Because you were supposed to take care of that already. That's why."

"I told you," Ajani said, rolling his eyes, "B don't mess with powder. He only fucks with weed."

"So what, yo? You've known him since you were fuckin' born," Pedro said. "Just ask him."

"No way. B would get pissed as hell if I asked him about that shit. Forget it."

"So ask Felix," Pedro insisted. "I'm tellin' you, bro. I'm sick of this nickel-and-dime shit we've been doin'. I'm workin' too hard for not enough pay. We need to step it up, yo. That way we can buy what the hell we want. *Do* what the hell we want."

"Why don't *you* ask Felix?" Ajani said.

"C'mon, man. You know why. We done gone over that shit, like, a million times," answered Pedro. "Those ninth-graders like you more."

"Yeah, I wonder why." Again Ajani and Chris Parker laughed it up.

Pedro was losing face and his patience. "Fuck you two, man. It's just 'cause you can play ball with them. That's why, yo."

Chris Parker added, "Yeah, and you can't, nigga. Ha-ha."

"Whatever, yo. Wait till I hit my growth spurt. I'm gonna be taller than both of you bitches."

"Doubt it. And your spic ass still won't be able to beat me on the court," Ajani said as he playfully elbowed Chris Parker in the ribs.

"Just fuckin' ask Felix like we talked about," Pedro demanded.

"I got ya." Ajani noticed it was getting darker. "I'm gonna bounce home. I'm starvin'."

"I'll see you tomorrow before school," Chris Parker said. "Peace."

Ajani slid back through the hole in the fence, grabbed his silver Mongoose behind the bushes, and headed home with money in his pocket. It took him just over five minutes to ride back over the expressway and to his mom's place.

When he got there, Ajani pulled out a key that hung on a dirty shoelace around his neck and unlocked the door to the one-bedroom apartment he shared with his mother, Dolores. The apartment was cramped for two, with minimal upkeep. That was problematic, but for Ajani it was home.

Earlier that morning, Dolores had prepared some chicken cutlets and corn niblets for him to reheat in the microwave. Ajani set up a tray in the living room and turned the boxy TV to ESPN. Then he turned on a fan. The air conditioner didn't work, but the fan gave the boy some relief from the heat and the stuffiness. Ajani went back to the kitchen and set himself up with an inviting plate of chicken, corn, and some instant mashed potatoes he whipped up on the stove. After pouring himself a glass of apple juice, he brought his meal into the living room.

The time on the basic cable box above the TV read 7:59. Ajani placed his napkin across his lap and watched *Top Plays of the Week* as he slowly ate, wishing that it were basketball season. Finishing his food, he threw his napkin onto the tray. A few minutes later, the door opened, and Dolores walked in, looking slightly inebriated.

"Hi, baby. How are ya?"

"Mama, I'm good. How are *you*?"

"Sore, baby." She unlaced her Keds and immediately sighed with relief. "Go get me my flip-flops from the bedroom."

Ajani ran into the other room, grabbed the orange flip-flops, and brought them into the kitchen.

"Thank you, honey. No one should have to stand up that many hours straight." She sighed and drearily said, "Did you like the chicken, baby?"

"Yes."

"Good. Did you do your homework?"

"Yes."

That was a lie, but it had been a couple of years since she had called his bluff.

"Good boy. Now go back in the other room. I'll be right there."

Ajani went to sit in the other room as his mother pulled out a pint of Jim Beam from a paper bag. She cracked the seal and took a whiff of the familiar smell. After filling her glass high over a handful of ice cubes, she snuggled up next to Ajani, and they watched ESPN together.

4

Primo and I arrived at a building on 17th Street, west of Union Square, and were quickly buzzed in.

"The buttons don't work at night," Primo told me as we stood in the elevator. "See." He repeatedly pushed the button marked 5. "It's locked. You need a key. Don't worry, though. She'll bring us up."

The elevator groaned and grumbled as it took us up to the fifth floor. The door slid open. Then a woman swung open a second steel door that led directly into her apartment.

"Hey, Penny. How are ya?" Primo asked.

Penny pushed up her glasses with her index finger and replied, "Hi, Primo. I'm well. C'mon in. And who's your friend over here?"

"This is B," Primo announced as we walked in and took a seat.

"Hello, B. How do you do?"

I nodded and gave a warm smile.

Penny cleared space off an old recliner and took a seat. A black-and-white cat quickly jumped on her lap. We were sitting nearby on a matching couch.

"So, Primo, tell me, how has life been?" she asked.

"Life?" Primo got a kick out of the generic question. "Life is like it's been since day one—pointless."

"Jesus Christ, Primo. What's up *your* butt today?" Penny stroked her hand through her disheveled gray-blond hair. "So morose."

"Just kiddin'," Primo said.

But I wasn't too convinced he was.

He pulled out a joint and waved it at Penny. "Ya mind?"

"Not at all."

Primo lit the joint slowly and deliberately. Inhale. Exhale. He repeated and then passed the joint to me. I took a big drag. Penny took the jay from me and began to puff.

I leaned back on the couch to take a quick scan of the spacious loft. It was in dire need of a makeover. "How long you been here, Penny?" I asked.

"Since '86. Can you tell? Back in the day you could buy a place like this for about twenty-five thousand. Union Square was different, though. I used to carry mace religiously. But now, not so much. I usually forget to put it in my purse."

"So, if you don't mind me asking," I continued, "how much did you have to put down?"

"Let's see. About twenty percent down, so that's—"

"Five thousand!" Primo blurted out. "Damn!" The two of us shook our heads in unison. "Can you believe that?" Primo said. "Five thousand down. That's *it?*"

"Yup. I had a few freelance editing jobs and was able to put together a tiny nest egg. I guess it's the best investment I ever made—except for my education, maybe. Anyway, I paid the place off a couple years ago. A freakin' twenty-year mortgage, but now I own this baby."

She spread her arms wide. The thick smoke dispersed throughout the loft, creeping up the enormous eleven-foot windows lined with long hanging ferns.

"Not the bank's. It's *mine*," she continued. "And thank Christ for that. Not so easy for you youngsters, is it? On my salary, I wouldn't be able to get something a third of this size nowadays."

"Do you ever think about selling?" I asked.

"What for?" Penny raised one eyebrow. "I have nowhere else to go. No, this is where my journey has brought me."

"What journey?" Primo asked.

"The one we all must take. Mine has led me right here. Right in front of you two. Right now."

Primo took a couple of hits and looked over at me. "B, she's stoned as fuck, right?" Smoke clouded out of his nostrils. "Old people get deep when they're high."

"Primo, don't be fresh," Penny said. "What I *mean* is that I love words, paragraphs, books—the art of writing. So I searched for that. That was a quintessential part of my quest. I sacrificed greatly for it, but in the end, I dig what I do. So all in all, I'm content. You see? You two will each have to figure out where your journey takes you. Or more accurately, where you each will take *it*." Penny leaned in as if about to say something very significant. "Always remember to observe the signs. If you ignore them for long enough, they'll vanish on you." She leaned back on the recliner and took a drag from the jay. "Yep. My city. My loft. My books. Simple. Just the way I like it. I don't see myself leaving here anytime soon." She softly stroked the top of her cat's head.

"Yeah," I said, thinking out loud. "I would just chill here till my dying days. A place like this is all I need."

"I wanna die on an island far from here," Primo said.

"Hopefully no one's gonna die anytime soon, alright?" said Penny. "So, let's see what you got."

Primo reached into his backpack, pulled out a medium-sized bag, and put it on the coffee table.

"Yum," she said. "How much?"

"Two grand."

"Two grand? Inflation isn't just for real estate now, is it? Not a problem, though. This will easily last me for months."

Penny pushed the cat off her lap and walked all the way back to her built-in bedroom. When she returned, she threw the money down on the table right in front of Primo. In her other hand, she was holding a thin stack of perforated loose-leaf papers that were clearly ripped from a notebook, and placed them on the table in front of me. I recognized the papers right away.

"I'd like to talk to you about what I read," Penny said, sitting down on her recliner once again and leaning back until the footrest popped out.

"Where... I mean... *how* did you get these?" I asked.

Penny was about to answer when Primo jumped in. "I brought 'em over, bro. I snatched 'em from your room a couple days ago. Don't get all huffy about it, aight? I did it outta love, homie."

"What would make you do somethin' like that, dummy? That's my private shit."

"Just relax, take a deep breath, and listen to the woman for a sec. Just trust me, aight?"

I wasn't comfortable with anyone reading what I write. No one. And here, on a stranger's coffee table, was a stack of my writing.

I looked over at Penny. "Why did he give that to you?"

"Probably because I work for a publishing company."

"Oh, yeah? Which one?" I was skeptical.

"Independent Think Tank," Penny answered.

"Never heard of it."

"We're small but still put out quite a decent amount of books and short story collections. I also teach writing classes at Columbia in the evening."

"So, what did you think?"

I had just put myself out there to be skinned alive, but I had never met a book publisher before, and she *did* read some of my intimate work.

"Actually, that's why I was pleasantly surprised when Primo brought you over."

The kettle on the stove whistled.

"Do either of you want some tea? I have a few different kinds— Lemon Zinger or Honey Vanilla Chamomile, I think."

"No, thanks," I said. Primo also shook his head.

She got herself a mug from the kitchen, put in a tea bag, and filled it to the brim with piping hot water. Gripping the mug with both hands, she brought it back to her seat, then blew on the top as the steam puffed out.

Her eyes locked with mine. Her tone was serious as she said,

"Truthfully, I'm not sure. I mean, this is like nine pages of a story. And it's not the beginning or the ending, either. It's right in the freakin' middle. Or at least I hope that's what it is." She peered at me through her glasses.

I confirmed her assumption with a nod.

"Your spelling is appalling, and, frankly, so is your punctuation."

As she spoke, I could feel my jaw clench. I started to reach for my papers, but Penny stopped my arm with a gentle hold.

"More important than all that," she said, "there's something deeper in there that I very much enjoyed. I haven't put my finger on it, but I can tell you that I've been doing this a long time. I've read many, many stories. And I'm telling you—there's something special hidden in your writing. It *is* hidden, though."

I shuffled the papers till they were neatly aligned. I had heard enough for one day.

"You ready, Primo? It's gettin' late. I gotta bounce."

Penny led us to the elevator and called it to her floor. The metal door clanked open, and the two of us got in.

"It was a pleasure, Primo," Penny said, winking at him. Turning to me, she added, "B, I hope we see each other again."

The elevator door slid shut with a bang.

5

The following morning, I headed out to Brooklyn in a lukewarm drizzle.

Me come from New Delhi.
Me not got no worry.
And if you fuck with me,
I'm gonna dash my curry.

M.I.A. was blasting from my iPhone as I rode the F train.

When I got above ground, I walked through the Fulton Street Mall. Heavy rain now peppered the pavement, but local shoppers were still out with ponchos, umbrellas, and boots.

Two blocks beyond the outdoor mall's bustling main strip, I turned left into a short dead end. On the near corner was a two-story brick building. Various colored orchids sat in the front windowsill of the laundromat on the first floor. The inside was spotless and well lit, but the rows of fluorescent tubes above me were too bright for comfort. Passing a man folding his whites on a table, I made it to the back and knocked on the door in front of me.

"Erro? Who is it?"

"It's me, Mrs. Robinson. It's B."

"Oh, hi, B. How ah you, honey?"

"Fine, Mrs. Robinson. How are you doing?"

I heard a buzz, followed by a click. I opened the heavy door and closed it behind me.

"I always tell you, B. You call me Lu Chu, okay?"

"Sorry, Lu Chu."

"You looking faw Chang?" She pointed to another room down the hallway. "He back there."

"Thanks, Lu Chu," I said.

"No probrem, B. You handsome thing, you."

Inside the room, I saw Chang sprawled out on the couch, watching a repeat of *UFC Fight Night*.

"Ouch. That had to hurt," he said. "This is violent stuff. But ya see the skills some of these fighters have? Oooh!" He grimaced. "That knee had to hurt. That's all *I* know."

"Who's winning?" I asked.

"Not sure. Gotta see their bank accounts."

He looked up from the 52-inch HDTV on the wall. "How's the world treatin' ya, B? Ya holdin' up?"

"You know. Getting by."

"Right, right. The question is, though, are you getting *yours*?"

"I guess it depends how you mean."

"The question was purposely vague, B. There are many ways in which you could be getting yours. And you not being able to think of at least one way instantaneously speaks volumes."

"Oh, yeah? How's that?"

"It tells me that you are *not* in fact getting yours." Chang's face was sober.

"Quit fuckin' with me, Chang. Damn."

He unfroze his serious look and broke out laughing. "Why would I do that, baby boy? It brings me too much joy." He burst into laughter again.

"Yeah, whatever, man. I got the real joy right in my jacket pocket."

"*Now* you're talkin', baby boy. Let's go downstairs and light up."

Chang led the way, looking suave in his royal blue silk brocade suit. As beautiful as it is, I've never thought I could pull off that look. At least, not the way Chang does, that's for sure.

I followed him down the stairs to his half-furnished basement, the other half was unfinished with thick cement walls and a gray epoxy floor. Chang's sanctuary.

He went over to a trunk in the furnished part of the basement and pulled out a Pyrex glass hookah that I had bought for him months ago. It was love at first sight. I packed the oversized bowl to the top. Each of us grabbed hold of rubber tubes extending off the body of the elegant hookah. Chang lit the bowl, and we puffed on the glass mouthpieces at the end of the tubes—puffing and puffing until I couldn't see Chang's dark African face anymore through the milky white smoke.

Chang is not African American, or at least not how most people think of it. He was born in Nigeria, but when he was three years old, his mother and three sisters traveled westward, crossed the Atlantic, and stayed with relatives in the Caribbean. That wasn't meant to last, though. A couple of years later, he told me, they made their way from Kingston to Brooklyn, looking for more opportunity. His mother remarried and Chang took on his stepfather's last name— Robinson. Where the name Chang came from, I have no idea.

If he had any accent, he'd lost it along the way.

"This is something I learned from the Rastafarians when I lived just outside Kingston as a child," he said, cupping his hand in front of his face and exhaling a huge hit. The smoke bounced off his hand and right back into his face. When it cleared enough for me to see him again, his eyes were as red as the devil's. But such a virtuous man is not to the devil's liking.

Hanging from a thick metal chain in the cool cement confines of the basement was a large, patched-up punching bag. Chang took a deep pull, put down his hookah tube, and walked over to the black bag. He posed a wide stance and started throwing out kicks and strikes, barking sharp, short Chinese words every time he hit the bag. His blows were quick and precise. After a while, he returned to the hookah, took the tube out of my hand, and put it down. "It's your turn, baby boy."

I made my way to the punching bag and stood in front of it with my eyes closed. Taking a couple of deep breaths, I tried to summon as much energy as I could. Crouching down into a wide stance, I let out a yell.

"Keeahh!"

I punched as hard as I could and then did a side kick, remembering to extend my toes outward.

Chang stroked his Fu Manchu, nodding at me with a look of pleasant surprise. "Not bad, my friend. Not bad at all. I'm glad to see that you're actually accepting some of the knowledge I've been transmitting in your direction."

"I have."

He put his arm around me. "Yeah, except for that weirdo stance you got into at the beginning. It looked like a yoga pose gone sour. Fucked-up Warrior Pose or somethin'."

"I guess." I smiled sheepishly.

"And you're too tense when you strike. Remember when we first met?"

"Sure. I was smokin' a spliff while you were practicing kung fu ten feet away at Prospect Park."

"Yeah, all that smoke was throwin' off my chi."

"If I remember correctly, we got silly stoned. And you wouldn't stop showin' me how to throw punches from horse stance."

"Remember what I told you?"

"To stay relaxed."

"To stay relaxed. Never let things get the best of you. Got me?"

"Yes."

"Well, in that case, pack that bowl up again, baby boy. Let's celebrate your progress."

Chang pulled out an antique pocket watch from his silk pants.

"Shit. I forgot I have an appointment."

"Oh, should I leave?" I asked.

"Nah, baby boy. Just stay here for a minute. Puff away. I'll be right back." His slippers barely made a sound as he nimbly climbed the stairs.

Less than five minutes later, Chang came back down by himself with a leather satchel under his arm. He went into the bathroom and closed the door behind him. I heard a click and saw part of the wooden wall in front of me pop out slightly.

Chang came back and swung open the hidden door, exposing a concealed room. It was not the first time I'd seen the custom-built safety deposit boxes. A steel wall of boxes painted all black, at least a hundred of them. Each one came with a number and two round locks. Impressive in an understated way.

Taking the leather bag from under his arm, Chang opened one of the many boxes, put the satchel inside, and locked up the safe. Then he closed the hidden door. It was sweet. Who would ever suspect that this place is down here?

Although Chang didn't allow anyone besides his wife down in the basement, he made an exception for me. I've never been sure why, but I've always taken it as a sign of respect and, probably more importantly, a sign of trust.

He picked up the hookah tube, and we puffed some more.

"How'd you get into kung fu in the first place, Chang?"

"I was a late bloomer, baby boy. It's been almost twenty years, but I can recall it like it was yesterday. I was in a bad place. No money. No prospects. Nada. One day I was walking by a dojo just a few blocks from here. I saw a bunch of people packed inside. Something drew me in. Like those sci-fi movies, ya know? Like a tractor beam pulled me in. I *had* to check it out."

"What was going on there?"

"This health nut and kung fu fanatic by the name of John Little happened to be lecturing that day. He was so impressive that I decided to wait for the class to end so that I could possibly pick his brain. Well, imagine my surprise when I found out that the man in front of me had close ties to Bruce Lee."

"No shit? I *love* his movies. The one with Kareem Abdul—"

"I know. He blinds Jabbar in *Game of Death*. More than a movie star, Lee was actually a gifted teacher in touch with the Tao. His kung fu was based on it."

"You've told me about Taoism before, but you're always so elusive," I said.

"The Tao is elusive by nature. Besides, I was takin' my time with you, baby boy. It means we get to chill more. Just so you know, though, kung fu isn't just fightin'—punches and kicks. It's a way of life. A certain way you carry yourself. In my case, it helped me to find inner peace and strength. That then led to personal success and happiness."

Chang pulled a paperback off the shelf. He knew exactly where it was among all the others, as if he had referred to it often. Handing me the white book, he said, "Little wrote this about Bruce Lee and his philosophies. It was published in '96. I got it when it first came out. Now I pass it on to you."

I grasped the book so we each had a hand on it. Rather than let go, Chang pulled me toward him. "Just promise me you'll read it," he said. "It's chock-full of wisdom. And when I say wisdom, I mean the kind that you can take with you and utilize every single day that you're alive. See what you think."

"I'm intrigued."

"So read the book."

"I will."

"Yeah, you better," he said, letting go. "I'm gonna test you later, ya hear? *And* I want it back, too. You're not the only one who needs those lessons." Chang winked and grinned. "Now let me buy some of that sticky-icky already, baby boy."

6

The sky cleared, allowing the sun to peek out. I packed away my raincoat. The air was still thick with dampness that quickly clung to my face, neck, and forearms.

A livery cab was out in front of the laundromat, waiting to take me to Williamsburg.

"Wythe and North 11th, please," I said.

"No problem, boss," the driver answered as we sped away.

I stepped out of the car in front of Brooklyn Bowl, avoiding the massive puddle on the corner. Across the street was a team of bearded, mustached, and inked-up hipsters smoking butts in front of a dive bar. They're probably in front of every dive bar in this hood. Shit, Willyburg is like holy Zion to a hipster.

The side door of the Bowl was propped open with a rock. I walked through the green room to the side of the stage. DJ PM was going wild on the turntables, flawlessly blending beats, going from hip hop to R&B to funk. Finally looking up and seeing me applauding, he hit the stop button on his Technics 1200.

"Not bad. Not bad at all," I said. "PM's still nice as ever."

"What up, son-son? You know I keep it crispy. How ya been?"

"I've been, I've been."

"Ha-ha. I hear that." PM dapped me up. "Come with me, homie."

I followed him backstage, locking the door behind me. "So what's been goin' on lately?" I asked.

"Ya know, man. Just grindin'. I'm actually openin' for Talib Kweli and Wiz Khalifa tonight. I had to run over here real fast to do the sound check."

"That's sick. Talib's a beast. So is Wiz."

"I know, man! Also I've been opening for Scram Jones on Thursdays at Greenhouse in TriBeCa. I'm tryin' to lock down a weekly gig downtown at Santos Party House, too. It's tough right now, though. Ya know? Hard to find that money."

"Hell, yeah," I said, nodding.

"Oh! Ya know what else? Crazy shit, man. Check this. The other day this kid tried to rob me. Yo, he was fuckin' young as hell. I mean, like fifteen or somethin'. He tried to sneak up behind me, but I smelled the pizza on this young punk's breath."

"So what did you do?"

"I elbowed this kid in the mouth, and he ran home bleedin'! He was a straight pussy." PM pulled out some vinyl from his record crate. "Besides that craziness, I can't really complain, B. I mean, the economy's still in the shitter, and the music industry fell apart, but somehow I'm still spinnin' gigs—makin' a little dough. Thank god for that. Anyway, what ya holdin'?"

I handed over a plump vacuum-sealed bag.

"Nice. What is it?"

"Neville's Haze. Yo, I *love* this shit. I have some other stuff, but I saved this for you. It tastes like flowers." I thought for second. "Actually, it tastes more like sweet pussy dipped in a bucket of potpourri."

"Nice, I like that taste. How much do I owe ya?"

"Thirty-two hundred for the half pound."

"Cool. That's what I assumed. I'll probably need more of whatever you got in, like, three days or so. Oh, yeah, and I want ya to have these records, too. There are some good fuckin' darts in that stack. Some Slick Rick. Tribe. Gang Starr. Some Wu. Ya know—just some unforgettables for the collection." He handed me the cash and a stack of vinyl. "The records are on me, B."

"Thanks," I said putting everything in my bag. "I gotta make moves. I'm busy tonight, so I can't make the show. But throw me a text before your next gig at Santos."

"Sounds good, my man. Stay outta trouble, ya hear?"

"Yeah."

As I exited through the side door, my iPhone buzzed in my pocket. It was Norah.

"Ma, how are ya?"

The voice through the phone was piercing. "How the hell do you *think* I am? You were supposed to be over for dinner last night. What the hell happened?"

"Sorry. I... I got caught up at a friend's place."

"Caught up at a friend's place? Are you kidding me, Byron? I told you I was cooking a meat loaf. It all went to waste."

"Ma, please don't get all dramatic on me. Anyway, I told you I don't eat meat anymore. Besides, Willis ate some with you, I'm sure."

"Oh, please. How much meat loaf can a six-year-old eat? Poor baby hasn't had much of an appetite since they put him on his new medication. They change his meds so often, I freakin' swear they don't even wait to see what really works. Anyway, positive thoughts, positive thoughts. Right?"

"Definitely."

"We've got to be optimists, Byron, 'cause it doesn't seem much use being anything else."

I had to agree. Some of the things Norah says have real truth in them.

"You coming over tonight for leftovers?" she asked.

"How about you make some pasta and garlic bread for me, and I'll see you in about thirty. Sound good?"

"You got yourself a deal, mister."

The L train brought me back to Manhattan in no time. I made

a pit stop at a liquor store and then walked to Norah's apartment in the Lillian Wald Houses. She's lived in the same two-bedroom apartment since I was a kid. Eleven flights up, packed into blocks of identical red-brick buildings in Manhattan's Lower East Side.

"Yo, Ajani!" I called out.

Ajani and his two friends were sitting on top of the monkey bars, eating Sour Patch Kids. When he looked up at me, I waved him over.

"Hey, B. What's goin' on with you?" Ajani asked after he closed the gate to the playground.

"I'm good. I'm just about to have dinner with Norah and Willis. You wanna come and get some pasta?"

"Thanks, but nah. I gotta go home in a bit and meet my mom."

Ajani grew up in the building next to my mother's. It wasn't uncommon for Norah to drag him up for a quick bite.

"You doin' good?" I asked. "You got any problems you need to talk to me about?"

"Nah. I'm all good."

"Okay, okay. Sounds good. When you wanna play some ball? I still owe you one from the beatin' you gave me last time."

"How about the day after tomorrow?"

"Perfect. So, I got you penciled in? Usual time?"

"Yep."

"Alright. It's on."

The boy went back to his friends, and I headed up to the eleventh floor.

Norah shared the place with my little brother Will. Willis Antonio Sully has a different father than me, but I've never thought of him as only half a brother. He's my whole brother, but in some ways more like a son. I couldn't imagine creating a kid in this fucked-up reality. But Will represents everything good in the world, untouched by society's rules and judgments. That doesn't mean he's unburdened. Less than seven years on this forsaken planet, and this poor kid has laid ill in a hospital bed more than anyone should in an entire lifetime. Hell, in *ten* lifetimes. Rule *numero uno*—life isn't fuckin' fair.

I opened the door with my key. I used to carry it on a dirty shoelace around my neck. An official latchkey kid.

"Look who it is," Norah said, standing there in a maroon sweat suit.

She poured tomato sauce over a bowl of tortellini and put a basket of garlic bread on the kitchen table. Home cooking.

I put my backpack down on the floor against the wall and gave Norah a kiss on the cheek. "Hey, I brought you this." I handed her a bottle of Long Island Merlot.

"What are you trying to do, get me drunk? You have bad news you wanna tell me? You can just tell me sober. I can take it."

"Ma, nothin's wrong. I just wanted to have a drink with ya."

She narrowed her eyes, as if trying to see directly through me. "What's in the book bag?"

"A book and some records." And about a pound of pot. "Don't worry about my bag, Norah."

"Okay, kiddo. I'll grab a couple glasses, the good crystal. I hide 'em in the back of the pantry."

"I know."

Willis came running into the kitchen. He must have finally heard my voice.

"Hey, guy. Give me a big one."

"Byyyyron!" he screamed as he jumped into my arms, squeezing tightly. It seemed like today was a *good* day for him. He was happy, not out of it.

"Let's eat some noodles, buddy."

"With extra sauce!" he squealed. "And I'm sitting next to *you*!"

I wanted to savor every bite, since I only get home cooking at Norah's. Once Will saw me dig in, he ate savagely, getting red gravy all over his chubby cheeks.

Norah and I easily killed off the Merlot and started working on a bottle of Pinot Grigio that she had opened when she got home after work at the hospital.

Half an hour later, Willis's eyelids were hanging heavy. The pasta had made him tired. I carried him to his room, gently placed him on his bed, and pulled his *Star Wars* blanket up to his chest. After I turned off the light, I walked back into the kitchen.

"He adores you," Norah said, lighting up a Capri Ultra Thin and taking a deep drag.

"I would hope so."

"No, you know what I mean. I mean, that kid *really* can't get enough of you, Byron. You should stop by here more often. It wouldn't kill you, ya know."

I grabbed my glass of wine. "Ma, please don't start. I come as often as I can. I swear."

"So, what've you been doing with yourself?"

"Workin', ya know?"

Norah raised an eyebrow. "No, I *don't* know. Why don't you explain it to me?"

"There's nothin' to explain. I'm just tryin' to maintain and pay my bills."

"How have you been covering your rent, Byron?"

"Ma, please."

"What? I'm just asking."

More like interrogating. Slowly and painfully pulling teeth.

She puffed her cigarette.

"I told you a thousand times. I've been doing freelance work with Primo. I write for websites and blogs that need new material."

That's what I had been saying since I left high school over a decade ago. Although somewhat true then, by now it's just pure rhetoric that I use when people ask for my occupation or how I pay my bills. I took a gulp of wine, finishing off my glass.

"With Primo, huh?" she mumbled cynically. I could tell she was sick of my bullshit story about writing for websites and blogs.

"Yes. With Primo."

"That boy gets more out there every time I see him. His mother would be rolling over in her grave. And Sharon was such a lovely woman."

"Will you stop being so dramatic, please?"

"No, no. I mean it. Same with your dad. And same with me.

If I were dead, god forbid, I'd be rolling over in my grave, too."

I swear, sometimes Norah says things that just barely make sense.

"Thanks, Norah. That's really nice."

"What should I say, Byron?" She took another drag. "I'm so freakin' proud of all the *nothin'* you're doing? Would your dead father, may he rest in peace, be proud of how you seemed to have lowered your expectations to the bare minimum?"

"I don't know. But apparently *you* aren't."

"I always tell you to go back to school. You're not too old, if that's what you think. And I always tell you, Byron, I'll pay for it if you go to a CUNY or SUNY. Even if I have to take out loans. That's how strongly I feel about it, Byron. Your dad and I always said we would do what our parents didn't by paying for our child's full education. We had to do it ourselves. Nursing school, your father's master's degree, not to mention raising you. It was tough. Real tough."

"I know. That's why I do things differently than how you did it. I wanna work smart, not hard."

"Byron, working hard isn't some curse, like you think. It's like you feel entitled. Your whole damn generation. Ya know, if everyone was like that, *nothin'* would get done."

"I don't know what to say. I'm just on a different path than you, ya know?"

How *could* she know? *I* didn't even know what I meant.

"Byron, I'm nervous. Your lifestyle makes me very uneasy. You come over here with your bag, probably filled with pot. Your clothes certainly reek of it. You have no job and no real prospects. I just want you to get a hold of yourself and do yourself a favor. You're playing with fire every day. Some nights are a ball, I'm sure. But, Byron, you're playing with fire. And one of these days, you're gonna get burned. Maybe burned badly. It's time to grow the hell up already."

She put out her Capri, stood up, and dumped her ashtray into the garbage.

I put my empty wine glass in the sink and ran some water in it.

"Ma, I gotta get goin'. Thanks for dinner."

"Thanks for the Merlot."

I grabbed my bag from the floor and put on my jacket.

"Thanks for the Pinot."

I gave Norah a kiss on the forehead and left.

7

My head was spinning, but I wasn't dizzy. I felt light. Airy. Free. Free of stress. I took deep, tranquil breaths.

I was hiding in the dark. Hidden in a room full of trashed youth. The only light I could really see was from the votive candles placed on all the round drink tables. The earsplitting house and dubstep tracks had drunken Jersey girls stepping on my feet as they made their way to the dance floor, but it didn't bother me. That's how I knew the E had kicked in.

"This DJ sucks," Primo said, sliding in next to me. "I swear this shit is, like, what robots fuck to when we're all asleep." He put two gin and tonics on the table as he looked at me. "Hey, at least the molly works, right?"

I said nothing.

"How ya feelin', kemosabe?"

"Good." I couldn't really get much more than that out of my mouth.

"Yeah, I bet." Primo pointed to the far corner of the room. "Yo, you see those two dimes over there?"

All the people on the dance floor were blocking my view, but I was able to catch a glimpse.

"Those two girls are comin' home with us tonight," he said.

"Says who?"

"Says *who?* Says *me!* I know the tall girl through my boy who manages the music studio in Vinegar Hill. She likes to hang over there. You could say she's kind of a studio groupie. I told her to come here and to bring a friend. It looks like she didn't disappoint."

I nodded in agreement. In reality, I could barely see an arm's length in front of me.

"C'mon. Let's finish these drinks and go over there," Primo said. "They're waitin' for us. I wanna introduce ya."

We threw back the gin and tonics in two quick gulps. The alcohol quenched my thirst, but only for a second.

Primo got up first and extended his hand to pull me up. I needed the help. I followed him to the other side of the smoky room toward the young ladies.

"Hey, Melina. How ya doin' tonight?"

"Good, Primo," the taller one answered, giving him a cute wink.

"What's your friend's name?" Primo asked.

"Sabrina."

"Sabrina and Melina? What the hell is that about?"

The two girls giggled.

"This is Byron. But pretty much everyone just calls him B," Primo added. "Rumor has it, his dick is eight inches long."

I could feel my face turn red.

Looking over at my partner in crime through shutter vision, I found it hard to stay focused. Primo, on the other hand, was fucked up but still composed. He always handled the drugs and alcohol with ease. Laying the charm on thick. Pushing ahead. Trying to get more trim.

I was just trying to get my jaw to stop shifting from side to side. Ecstasy is in no way one of my favorite drugs, but that's how it goes sometimes. Some days, it doesn't really matter what drug it is. I just want to get high. There it is. My bottom line. I'm no dope or meth head. No barfly or pill-muncher. My theory is, why limit yourself to one thing? Since I was a teen, I've binged compulsively, trying everything. The main purpose of doing all those drugs? To conquer pain and the always lurking enemy—boredom.

Narcotics have taken me to places I've never been. Through the wormhole and back. But there's usually a price to pay. And I notice that more, every year that passes. Drugs used to be shiny, exciting, and mysterious. Mental alchemy. Not so much anymore. The sheen has dulled. The mystique is gone. But despite all that, to this day, I still crave the feeling of leaving my sober skin to head for greener pastures. In the search for serenity, some people bowl, or build model airplanes, or go antiquing, or crap like that. Not me. I get high.

Primo pulled his fitted Yankees cap down on his brow so that you could barely see his dilated pupils. He was already in mid-conversation with the girls when I was finally able to focus on the discussion.

"... is the best. Her skin? That ass? I wish that's what *my* legs looked like," Melina was saying to her friend.

Sabrina chimed in, "I know. I'm obsessed with her new video. Shakira rules!"

I looked over at Primo as if to say, *Why are you putting me through this?*

He gave me a look I had seen before, which said, *Hey, fuck it. Just follow my lead.*

With that, we ordered four rounds of Patron Silver, chilled. Glass after glass went down like water. I rubbed lip balm on my dry mouth.

"What kind is that?" Sabrina said, putting her hand on my thigh and looking into my wide eyes.

"Desert Essence, with jojoba oil and aloe vera." I felt stupid saying that out loud. I don't even know what jojoba oil is, but it works great.

The petite brunette squeezed my thigh and blurted out, "No way! I love that stuff!"

From that point on, I knew what was going to happen.

After Sway finished last call, Sabrina and I ended up on my bed. I pulled the shades to block the morning rays that would be finding their way into the apartment. We made out for a while. Curtis

Mayfield played from my laptop in the background. The sexy, fair-skinned brunette stood up to face me, pulled her black dress over her head, and threw it at me. Then she gave me a look that all women have given men since the dawn of time. The look they give right before they are about to take what they want from you.

Looking at me with her temptress eyes, she slid her black thong down her creamy thighs. I stared in front of me, my vision slowly improving. There Sabrina was, naked except for her black stilettos.

"You wanna fuck me in my heels, Mr. Man?"

8

"For Christ's sake," I said, as I removed my eye mask. My eyes could barely open until I wiped the gross, dried-up goobers from the inner corners. My mouth was terribly dry. Coarse sandpaper. I could still taste the liquor lingering on the back of my tongue. I burped up some burning bile.

Sabrina was already gone by the time I woke up. I think she kissed me on the cheek before she left, but it might have been a dream.

My iPhone had four voicemail messages. When we got back from the club after sunrise, I thought I had heard it vibrating somewhere, wedged in the sofa cushions. But with the Stunning Sabrina entertaining all morning, I couldn't help ignoring the buzz.

Before checking my voicemails, I grabbed a roll of Tums from the kitchenette, bit off two, and took a huge swig of water.

The first message was from Norah. "Byron, your brother's in the hospital! We're at Gouverneur! Come soon!"

The second message was from Norah again. "Byron, where the hell are you? Byron, Willis isn't doing well at all. Please hurry."

And the third. "Byron, the doctors say they have to do emergency surgery. They say there's fluid pushing up against his brain, and they have to drain it. I'm scared. Please hurry."

There was a long silence at the beginning of the fourth message.

Finally Norah spoke. Her voice was not piercing but sorrowful. I could barely make out her words through all the whimpering and sniffling. "Byron, he's dead. Will's dead. They couldn't save my baby." There was more whimpering. "He's gone."

My phone dropped to the floor. Blood left my face, giving me the spins. I had to sit down. I was breathing so heavily, yet felt helplessly breathless. I was hyperventilating. My muscles tensed tightly as I went blank.

The next thing I knew, my mind was lucent. The storm of horrible news had violently smashed through my head, leaving calm yet eerie waters. I had to call Norah. She was probably alone—alone, wondering why the men in her life always leave her. In one way or another, they all did. My biological father died in a car crash. There was that shithead Tucker Sully, poor Willis's dad. He knocked up my mother and skipped town, but not before using her debit card to settle a nasty little tab with a bookie.

And now Willis, bless his beautiful soul, had left her as well.

Then there's me, Byron Bella. The last man standing in Norah's life. And I'm not even there for her. My mother has no shoulder to cry on. Some son, huh?

9

I DON'T KNOW WHAT I MAY SEEM TO THE WORLD.
BUT AS TO MYSELF I SEEM TO HAVE BEEN ONLY
LIKE A BOY PLAYING ON THE SEASHORE AND
DIVERTING MYSELF NOW AND THEN IN FINDING A
SMOOTHER PEBBLE OR A PRETTIER SHELL THAN
THE ORDINARY, WHILST THE GREAT OCEAN OF
TRUTH LAY ALL UNDISCOVERED BEFORE ME.

— LAST WORDS OF SIR ISAAC NEWTON

I REMEMBER, ABOUT A YEAR AGO, I TOOK
WILL TO LONG BEACH. HE WORE A GILLIGAN HAT
WITH A CHINSTRAP, MATCHING KHAKI SHORTS, AND
SANDALS.
THE SUN WAS SHIMMERING DOWN ONTO THE
CHOPPY ATLANTIC. WE WALKED ALONG THE
CROWDED BOARDWALK HAND-IN-HAND. NORAH WAS
ADAMANT ABOUT NOT GIVING WILLIS JUNK FOOD,
BUT I COULDN'T RESIST. WE ATE FUNNEL CAKES
AND CHERRY SNOW CONES. WILL'S MOUTH WAS
COVERED IN STICKY RED SYRUP.
MY BROTHER HAD JUST HAD A GRUELING
SURGERY A FEW WEEKS EARLIER. STUCK WITH
NEEDLES IN HIS PALE LITTLE ARM, FED GAS, AND

CUT OPEN. NOT THIS PARTICULAR DAY, THOUGH. ON THIS GORGEOUS DAY, WILLIS PUT ASIDE HIS ILLNESS TO PLAY AT THE BEACH.

WE HEADED TO A STRIP OF BLACK ROCKS THAT START ON THE WET SAND AND EXTEND INTO THE SEA. ONCE WE GOT DOWN THERE, THE COOL SALTY WATER RUSHED OVER MY FEET, GIVING RELIEF.

WILLIS WAS BUSY HUNTING FOR SHELLS, WHEN HE NOTICED A FLOCK OF SANDPIPERS. WE SAT ON THE ROCKS TOGETHER AND WATCHED THE TINY BIRDS FEED.

THE PIPERS WOULD WAIT FOR EACH DANGEROUS WAVE TO RECEDE INTO THE OCEAN. WITH THEIR FEET A MERE BLUR, THEY WOULD MOTOR DOWN TO THE WET SAND TO SEE WHAT THE WAVE HAD BROUGHT IN OR UNEARTHED. THEY WOULD SWIFTLY YANK A CRUSTACEAN OR BEETLE FROM THE SAND AND THEN SPRINT AWAY BEFORE THE FOAMING OCEAN'S EDGE ROLLED IN AGAIN.

WILLIS WASN'T SO DIFFERENT FROM THOSE PIPERS. BOTH HE AND THE BIRDS WERE JUST TRYING TO SURVIVE BETWEEN EACH CRASHING WAVE THAT NATURE THREW AT THEM.

WE CREMATED HIM THREE WEEKS AGO. NORAH LET ME TAKE MOST OF HIS REMAINS TO SPREAD. SOME I LEFT IN A SIMPLE URN AT HER APARTMENT, SOME I SCATTERED BY HIS SCHOOL PLAYGROUND, BUT MOST I TOSSED OFF THE STRIP OF BLACK ROCKS INTO THE ATLANTIC. THE PIPERS WATCHED FROM A DISTANCE AS THEY SCURRIED TO FIND FOOD BETWEEN THE BREAKERS AND FOUGHT TO LIVE ANOTHER DAY.

I closed my journal and started to twist a blunt. The Afgoo was frosty and sticky as sap. The strip of water-pressed bubble hash I added to the center guaranteed an extra kick. I needed it. Each hit was thick and powerful. My lungs filled, but the smoke kept expanding until I coughed it all out.

I've been trying not to think about my brother, but the wound is still fresh and stinging. To my surprise, though, something else has been stirring in the pot besides misery. Gratefulness. Blessed to be breathing. Will's brief battle with cancer took *his* life, not mine. Mine is still intact, ready for another shot at the wet sand in between those unforgiving waves.

I'm ready to accomplish my dreams and experience fulfillment. But first I have to cover my rent, which is due in less than a week. Rent in Manhattan can easily make you forget about dreams and fulfillment and shit like that.

I put out the Dutch, locked up, and left my building. Time to hit the pavement. I had to make my way to midtown to collect a debt.

When I got off the F train at 42nd Street, I headed up the block and stopped in front of a green-and-yellow awning, stained from years of hanging in the city's soot. The words *Bengal Halal Restaurant* were printed in white letters. I walked in, and tucked way in the back, in a black leather jacket, was just the man I came to see.

"Hey, B. How's it hangin'?" he asked.

"Franky Golden," I said. "Where the fuck you been hidin' out? Besides this dump."

"Dump?" Franky put down his fork and looked at me as if I had just insulted his dead grandmother. "Dis place might not look like much to the layperson," he said in his thick New York Italian accent, "but the food's clean. Dese guys got all kinds of rules for what they put in their mouths. All their food passes tests, ya know. Dat's why I told ya to meet me here." He picked up his fork and dug in again.

I sat down across from him. Franky was thin as hell, but gobbled his meal as if he hadn't seen food for days. As he chewed with his mouth open, he smacked his lips. What remained of his stringy black hair was slicked back. His face was leathered like his jacket from years of Marlboros.

Golden finished his last bite and wiped his face with the napkin he had tucked in his collar. He threw the napkin on his empty plate and gulped down a can of Dr. Pepper. Without shame, he let out a bellowing belch.

"So, what's up?" he asked. "Ya got some chains for me?"

"Nah, man. I was wonderin' where my cash was."

"Oh, yeah. I forgot about dat."

"I didn't."

Franky smiled. "Don't worry, guy. Ya know I always got ya. What's the numba again?"

"Eight-fifty."

"Oh, yeah? Hmmm. You wouldn't want a new MacBook instead, would ya?"

"No. I already got one of those from you. Plus, I need the dough."

Franky reached into his worn jacket, pulled out some money, and quickly counted it. Handing me the cash under the table, he said, "When I was your age, you could buy a couple lids for fifty bucks."

"Yeah, but it was mainly sticks and seeds and probably dragged through the dirt. The shit you get from me is chronic."

"True," Franky said.

I stood up and shook his hand goodbye.

While still gripping my hand, he said, "I heard about your baby bro. I just wanted to let ya know I'm sorry, pal."

"Thanks."

"He was a cute kid. I know ya loved him. He's in a betta place, though, right?"

"Wherever he is, at least there's no more hospital gowns, ya know? I guess that counts for somethin'."

Franky nodded. "Yeah, it does count for somethin'. See ya around, B."

"Take care, Franky."

I headed to the front of the restaurant.

"Ya don't want any halal food, B?" Franky called from the back.

"No," I answered.

"You're missin' out! Get me some chains, B! Eighteen karat! Gold's skyrocketin'! You got my numba!"

I walked out without responding.

Franky carried a jeweler's scale in his back pocket, so he was prepared to weigh gold at any moment. He would bust out the digital scale right smack dab in the middle of the sidewalk if it could make him a buck.

One of my favorite Franky stories was the time he actually convinced this Mexican worker on a construction site to give up his four gold fillings. The amount he gave the Mexican for the fillings varies, depending on who's telling the story, but I sure as hell know that Franky Golden made a nice little profit for himself. He always does—like any professional hustler. Franky would get his hands on all kinds of things, from La-Z Boys to Louis Vuitton luggage. But like his adopted name suggests, the man specializes in gold.

He once told me that every other week or so he would go to the Diamond District to meet his connect. His buyer, who Golden so lovingly and simply calls "the Jew," would check out the goods and always pay in crisp bills. Franky promised to take me to meet the Jew someday soon because of the guy's apparent infatuation with heady pot.

Perhaps Golden shouldn't be trusted. Hell, he'd sell bullets to a baby. But I like him anyway. His ear's to the street. And he knows everything. That's invaluable in my line of work.

10

"Pass! I'm open!" shouted Ajani.

His teammate chucked the ball across the court. Ajani caught the pass and went in for a reverse lay-up with ease.

"Nice play, lil' man," said another teammate.

Ajani stood with his hands on his hips, catching his breath as sweat dripped off his face onto the dry black pavement. He was smaller than the freshmen and sophomores on the court, but not one of them could match his heart or skill.

Ajani still used the ball his mother had given him when he was nine. After countless hours of dribbling and shooting, the gripping on the ball had become worn and polished, so it was now smooth as an egg.

"Mine! Mine!" Ajani called as he dove to the pavement to grab the ball. He then passed it between his opponent's legs. One of his teammates caught the ball and violently dunked it with a tremendous roar. With that point, the game was over. The two exhausted pickup teams dapped each other up and packed their things to leave.

"Yo, Ajani, that pass between the legs was murder," said Felix. "Yo, did you catch how upset that chump was? If he wasn't so black, that nigga's face woulda been red as a muthafucka. I swear, every time you play with us, you got another trick up your fuckin' sleeve."

Ajani didn't say anything.

"You don't talk much, do ya?" Felix said. "You ain't a bragger, I can tell."

"I just practice a lot. That's all."

"Oh, okay. That's some real talk right there."

It was another muggy August day in the city. Felix wiped his face with a towel, took off his soaking-wet white undershirt, and put on another just like it. He also pulled out a brown bag that was wrapped tight and taped all around. "It's three-fifty," he said.

"I thought an eight ball was only three-hundred," said Ajani.

"Yeah, to some. But you gotta *earn* those type of prices. Let's just say that you're lucky that I'm such a good guy to even help your ass out with this shit. What are you, like, ten?"

"Twelve." Ajani's face went sour. He hated looking so young.

"Oh, sorry, lil' man. Don't get all bent outta shape, lil' homie. I'm just fuckin' with ya. So we got a deal? Three-fifty?"

As the sun beat down on Ajani's face, he squinted and wiped away some sweat. "Yeah, we got a deal."

He pulled out three hundred dollars in a rubber band, grabbed another fifty from his money clip, and handed the cash to Felix. Then he took the stash from the older boy and stuffed the paper bag in his sock.

"If you get popped with that shit, you don't fuckin' know me," Felix said. "You don't say my name. You don't even remember my fuckin' existence." He raised his right hand, showing his large fist. "I will fuckin' break your face up if you fuck me like that, nigga. Ya got me?"

Ajani's look went sour again. "Yeah, I got ya."

"It's business, Ajani, nothin' personal." Felix opened his fist and gently put it around Ajani's narrow shoulders. "Remember that. It's the first rule in this business you gettin' in. Never personal. Understand?"

Ajani nodded.

"I like you," said Felix with his arm still fastened around the boy. "Just be smart. No fuck-ups. Best be on your A-game."

Felix gave him a soft punch on the arm, and the two parted.

11

Primo and I boarded the 33-footer docked on the Hudson. The name painted on the back of the pristine boat read:

Angelfish

It was so bright on deck that my extra-dark aviators barely shaded my eyes.

Chilly was sitting in the back, smoking a fat joint as he normally did, looking content in his white captain's cap and matching white nautical flood pants and button-down.

"Hey, hey. How's it hangin'?" he called, raising the hand that held the smoking joint. "Come back here and take a seat with me."

When we sat down beside him, he passed me the giant spliff. I ashed it into the river and took a few puffs.

"Chilly, this is my boy, Primo," I said.

"The infamous Primo, huh? Heard many a story, buddy. Welcome to my humble hangout."

"It ain't so humble," Primo said, looking around. "The only boats I got are for the bathtub."

We all laughed. I glanced at the window to the living quarters and saw a sexy black woman, naked as could be. After putting her long straightened hair into a bun and slipping into a cream-colored robe, she looked over and caught me staring at her. I turned away quickly, but saw that Chilly had also caught me.

"Like what you see, B?" Chilly asked.

I laughed awkwardly.

"Yeah, well," said Chilly, "that's *mine* right there. We'll find out if she's got a couple sisters." He smacked his leg as he laughed loudly.

The woman in the robe emerged. "Hello, boys. What's so funny?"

"Nothin', sweetie," Chilly answered. "Can you make us a fresh pitcher of margaritas? And turn up the tunes! Let's all let our hair down for while!"

"Of course, baby," she said, turning up the oldies.

Between glasses of margaritas, we took shots of Don Julio 1942 with salt and lime.

"Looks like today is all about tequila," proclaimed Chilly, tipping his captain's hat.

"Couldn't ask for more," I said.

Joints were passed around for an hour. Occasionally, a tour boat or small motorboat passed by and faded away just as serenely as it had appeared. A few people were quietly sunbathing on some of the other boats that were docked nearby. But it felt like we had the river to ourselves.

Once again, we licked salt off the back of our hands, guzzled another round of shots, and bit on lime wedges to finish the routine. My vision was definitely starting to blur.

Chilly's woman got up from his lap and headed inside. "Later, boys," she said as she briefly looked back at us. "I'm gonna take a little beauty nap."

"You don't need one of *those*, baby," said Chilly. "I can tell ya that."

I enjoyed her perfect hourglass figure as she walked away. It took me a bit to snap out of my trance.

Chilly handed me another giant joint.

"How long you been smokin' ganja?" I asked him.

"Since I was eleven. I never smoked a cigarette a day in my life.

But I can't imagine a day without good ol' Mary Jane."

"You think you're still in pretty good shape?" I asked. "I mean, do you think it's damaged your lungs?"

"I just had a checkup, and I'm as healthy as a horse. Or should I say a fish? That's what I am, ya know? I love the water—being in the water. It keeps me young. Shit, we *are* mainly water." Chilly puffed on the huge jay. "Look, I think if you stay with good pot, and maybe some shrooms once in a while to keep you humble, you'll be all good. In fact, marijuana has many healing properties. It's a miracle plant with many benefits. It can relieve pain and cure ailments."

"Is it true that no one ever died from pot?" Primo asked.

"Actually," said Chilly, taking a long drag from the joint, "there is that one case."

"Really?" Primo and I asked in unison.

"Yeah. Fifty tons of the shit fell on this guy's head. Made him flat as a pancake."

Again, we laughed it up.

Chilly pulled out a burgundy velour pouch, which made a clanking sound as he plopped it on his lap. He untied the strings, opened the pouch, and pulled something out.

"You ever see anything like this?" he said, handing me a round metal object. It had a lion stamped on the front. The back had a square-shaped indentation in the center. The surface was cool and polished.

"No," I said, handing the coin over to Primo. He held it up, allowing it to glisten in the sunlight.

"It's old currency," Chilly said. "Made from electrum, an alloy made from a mix of gold and silver."

"White gold, right?" Primo asked.

"Yep. With traces of copper and other metals as well," Chilly said.

"Where's it from?" I asked.

"The coins are Lydian," Chilly said, jiggling the pouch. "They're from what used to be called Asia Minor. Now it's Turkey. I've done a bunch of excavations all around the Mediterranean. Worked in all those countries, digging for booty — Spain, Morocco, Algeria, Egypt, Italy." He passed the cone-shaped spliff and continued, "Done 'em all. I try to get away as much as possible, boys. When we're not searching for treasure, we get to do some sightseeing. The trick is, you gotta blend in with the culture, ya know? You gotta be one of 'em. A local. Or else it's just not as fun."

"This must be, like, hundreds of years old," Primo said, examining the coin closely.

"Twenty-six hundred, to be specific," Chilly said. "Some say these are the first coins ever made."

"They must be priceless, right?" I asked.

Chilly nodded. "They *are* priceless, B. On the other hand, even the priceless usually has a price." He winked. "And some of them sure are mint."

"How are they in such great shape?" I asked, puffing on the cone and blowing clouds into the open sky.

"Curiosity. I like that, B. I found them at a shipwreck off the coast of Cyprus. It was a ship from the ancient world. I've worked on a bunch of these kinds of wrecks over the years. I was clearing away some sediment from part of the buried ship, when I saw —"

"Saw what?" Primo anxiously interrupted, like a kid hearing a suspenseful bedtime story.

"A chest," Chilly said, pleased that he had aroused his listeners' interest. "I could tell it was special from the moment I laid eyes on it. We found a lot on that trip. Most of it we gave to the Turkish government. But the chest came with me, if you know what I mean, jellybean."

"How many of these were in the chest?" I asked.

"Twenty-three. I keep them in this pouch for now 'cause, well, it's damn easier than lugging them around in a chest, ya know? Pretty soon, I'll put them away in a safe to hide out for a few years." He said this with a drunken grin.

Primo handed the coin to Chilly, who put it back with the others in the burgundy pouch, pulled the strings tight, and slid it back under his seat.

"So you wanna see the treasure I brought for *you*?" I asked.

"Hell, yeah," Chilly answered.

I threw a fluffy bag of weed with red hairs and forest-green leaves in front of him.

"Sweet Island Skunk," I said. "It's a bomb sativa."

"Well," said Chilly, "I've visited a lot of islands, boys, but I've never been to this one. Let's get smokin'!"

12

The next day at dusk, I saw my connect over by the Holland Tunnel.

Right after, I met up with Primo at the bodega next to his apartment, across the street from Tompkins Square Park. The humidity was thick, but that didn't discourage all the junkies from posting up on their usual benches. Or the yoked-up dudes puffing on Newports from doing workout regimens in the kiddie playground.

"Two Vanillas, please," Primo said to the Korean cashier. He looked back at me and said, "Two Dutches and a Red Bull — breakfast of fuckin' champions."

"Um, more like dinner time," I said, settling for a Martinelli's and a ripe banana.

"Fuck it. Time is just a number, B."

"Sank you veddy much," the Korean cashier cheerily shouted out. "See you tomado."

"I think we've bought enough blunts in there to put that guy's fuckin' kids through college," Primo said on the way out.

After the two of us walked into his pad, Primo immediately said, "Yo, you got that?"

"Yup. Check it."

Primo stuck his face into a big bag of Kush. "Yeah. This is what I'm talkin' about. It's got some stank on it."

"And there are a few strains to sample in the other small duffle. So we could try out what will be around next time, ya know? See what we like and what we don't."

"Lovely." Primo smelled the big bag of weed once more. "Your boy did it again. Your *secret* connect."

"C'mon," I said, starting to pack a bong hit. "We really gonna have this convo again?"

"Nah, we ain't gotta get into any conversation about that shit. We know where we at with that. We're supposed to be doin' this together, right?"

"Yeah," I said, hitting the bong.

"It works best if we both know all the people we're dealin' with, so there's never a problem, right?"

"Yeah."

"But for some reason you wanna keep me in the dark about who's hookin' us up?"

"It ain't like that, Primo," I said, shaking my head. I handed him the bong. "I don't wanna burn this bridge, so I'm just followin' instructions. He said he doesn't wanna meet anyone else except me."

"Yeah, I got ya," Primo said, taking a bong hit. "We both move the herb that comes through, yet I gotta be clueless about where it's comin' from."

"I'm just tryin' to handle this shit the right way, so we can both make dough."

"Word," Primo said. "I got ya loud and clear."

"Good."

"So we gonna hit up this party in NoHo? Let's do it. And bring some of that Kush, aight?"

When we got out of the cab, Primo walked to the front of a long line. He said his name to a girl with the VIP list, and she let us in right away. A freight elevator took us and four other people up to the top. The huge penthouse had 30-foot-high ceilings with oversized skylights that allowed the moon and starlight to penetrate.

A sexy Puerto Rican named DJ Morena was spinning records on a raised stage that looked like it had been built just for her. She was playing one of my favorites—"Apache" by the Incredible Bongo Band. A crew of five break-dancers was working it out on the linoleum. Photographers vigorously snapped away as the hyped-up crowd surrounding the b-boys chanted and cheered. Primo and I bobbed our heads to the classic breakbeats.

Eventually, we made our way to the back of the loft and walked single file up a narrow black spiral staircase. Primo opened the French doors at the top and led the way outside to a massive deck with three different levels. Well-kept tulip gardens and young Japanese maple trees in clay pots were strategically placed everywhere.

Beauties with beach balls giggled and splashed each other in an inlaid circular pool. I bent down and dipped my hand into the water. Heated.

"Vapor hit?" a voice said from behind.

I stood up next to Primo.

"Scott, what's up, buddy?" Primo said. "Thanks for the invite. I haven't seen you in a while. Where you been?"

"Out of the country mainly," replied Scott, a well-built man, about six-foot-six. His hair was combed perfectly, with not one strand out of place, and his face was clean-shaven. Pleated pants, a striped button-down, and a sports coat completed the look. I felt like a schlep next to him, but I have a personal rule never to wear pleated pants. Not even for a wedding or a funeral.

"May I?" Primo asked, reaching for the vapor pen.

"Of course," Scott said.

"Outta the country, huh? Where?" Primo asked after a few puffs from the pen.

"Switzerland, Iceland, Sweden. Basically the whole Nordic region," Scott answered. He took a long vapor hit. "Have you ever been? To the Nordic region?"

We both shook our heads.

"You have to go one of these days, boys. It's very pleasant during the summer months. I was showing the watch line out there to some clients, and I decided, fuck it, I'll make a vacation out of it. So I rented a Harley and just rode. And when I wasn't riding, I was at a hotel having three-ways. Shit. *Four*-ways."

"Sounds like a rockstar," Primo said.

"Primo, who is this you brought with you?"

"My business partner B," Primo said.

"B, huh?" He stuck out his hand. His grip was firm. Practiced. "Nice to meet you. I'm Scott. Hope you're enjoying the spectacular views from up here."

"We are," Primo said.

"B, have you tried one of these pens yet?" Scott asked. "They taste delish."

"Not yet. Seen them online, though. They're for smoking wax or oil, right?"

"The future of smoking, I assume," Scott said. "Here. Just press this button."

I pressed the button, took a pull, but couldn't tell if I was getting a hit until I exhaled a thin, light cloud. So velvety. So incredibly tasty. Wax was not like smoking any weed I had ever tried. The high was extraordinarily clean, yet quite overpowering. And the pen just accentuated those qualities.

"Perhaps the future," Scott continued. "But I still predict people are always going to want good old-fashioned flower, too. Speaking of which, did you bring any flower, fellas? I'm dying to see."

"I got *this*," I said, holding a bud up in front of me.

"That is crystally stuff," said Scott. "Impressive. Without question."

He pulled out a paper. Taking the bud from me, he crushed it in his hand and quickly rolled it up. Then he lit a match.

"Yo, hold up for a sec," I said, pushing his hands down. "You see that guy in black over there?"

A mean-looking muscular man in all black was staring right at us.

Scott laughed. "B, don't worry. That's Harry. He doesn't give a shit. In fact, I pay his ass. Primo, you didn't tell him?"

"Nope."

"This is *my* party," Scott said. "Those are my watches on the break-dancers downstairs. Did you notice?"

"No, I must've missed that."

"Yeah. They're doing a shoot to promote my upcoming line. So, anyway, definitely don't worry about Harry, okay? He's a uniformed cop during the day. But he gets paid shit, so I hook him up with some extra pay when I throw these little soirées from time to time. I just tell him to pretend like we're in Amsterdam—hell, *New* Amsterdam. The security isn't here to bother weed smokers, B. They're here to keep drunk invited guests in line and drunk *uninvited* guests out of the goddamn building."

Scott waved at Harry and made a silly face. Harry just looked in another direction, chewing on some kind of dried root.

"Can I interest any of you in a lollipop or a hand-dipped chocolate?" said a busty blonde in a black corset and a tray of treats strapped around her neck.

"Edibles have come a long way since your grandpa's pot brownie," Scott said. "Eat up."

Primo and I wolfed down some chocolates. We also made sure to take some lollipops for later.

The woman in the corset gave us a sweet smile and moved on to the next partygoer with her tray of tantalizing treats.

"Now, shall we?" Scott said. He lit the joint with a fresh match.

The three of us took turns puffing, taking our time.

Scott let out a little cough on the second round. "What the hell *is* this stuff?"

"The Snush," I answered.

"The *Snush*?" Scott asked.

"Yeah," I said. "Snoop Kush."

"Snoop has his own strain now?"

"Yup," Primo said. "And it's strong as fuck, aight."

"That's one way to put it," Scott said. "I'll take a pound. Most of it's for some buddies of mine. They're actually not buddies, they're jerk-offs, but they're *my* jerk-offs, so I like to keep them happy. Besides, I just like having some high-quality product around. You know why?"

"Why?" I asked.

"Hello? The bitches! C'mon, dudes. What's wrong with you two? That's what it's about—yourself and pussy. Don't forget those words of wisdom from your friend Scotty Wotty. Your fine self and some fine pussy. Understand?"

"Pussy's good," Primo said.

"Harry!" Scott shouted over to the bouncer chewing on a root. "Harry! Tell the DJ I wanna hear some Snoop D-O-Double-G next! Go and tell her!"

Harry nodded and headed in.

"As I was saying, let's start with a pound," Scott said to us. "And make sure you don't pull the old bait-and-switch on me." He nudged Primo's shoulder. "I'm joking, I'm joking! I know you'll do me right. Can I get that in the morning?"

"Sure," Primo answered. "It's seventy-two hundred."

"Wonderful," said Scott. "Exciting. Oooh, I think I have a hard-on."

Primo and I looked at each other, eyebrows up.

"I kid, I kid! I'm *kidding*, you guys!" Scott ashed over the side of the building. "I just got a brilliant idea. When's the last time you guys had a massage?"

Again we looked at each other with eyebrows lifted.

"I could use a rubdown," Scott said. "It's on me. What do you say? Let's link in the A.M. around ten. I know a spot in Chinatown. Don't worry. It's a nice place. Clean. Trust me. I'll text Primo the address. For now, I have some bottles that need to be popped. Come with me."

We followed Scott back inside to the kitchen, where we enjoyed two bottles of Dom Pérignon 1998 and many, many more vapor hits. By midnight, I was stumbling out of the party with the hiccups.

I don't remember getting back to my place, but I do remember puking out the window of a yellow cab on the way home.

13

At 9:15, my cell phone was buzzing with a text from Primo. The morning had come sooner than I had hoped. I jumped in the shower, got myself dressed, and checked the weather on my MacBook. Sunny for now but with a strong chance of showers. Life in a nutshell.

My burps still tasted like ganja chocolate and a hint of expensive champagne. Putting on my shades, I grabbed a brown Bloomingdale's bag and headed out the door.

Primo was not meeting us at the massage parlor. According to his long-winded text, he was laid up in bed, thanks to the Dom P we were guzzling the night before. He had brought home DJ Morena, and apparently she was not impressed with his hurling in the bathroom. Nevertheless, he forwarded me the address and told me to take care of things.

When I walked into the parlor, Scott was there, bright-eyed and bushy-tailed, waiting to greet me. He had drunk more and stayed out later than I had, but here he was, ready to rock. I was ready to croak.

"This is gonna be fun!" Scott proclaimed. "Let's do this!"

We walked back into the locker room, took a quick rinse, and put on plush white robes and slippers.

Scott peeked around to see if we were alone and said, "Here's my key." He admired himself in the mirror. "The cash is in my pants pocket. Just leave the bag in my locker."

I nodded.

"I'll meet you upstairs," he said, as he finished examining his nose hairs.

"Sounds good."

After he walked out of the room, I quickly transferred the Bloomingdale's bag from my locker to his and the knot of hundreds from his locker to mine. Then I swished around some complimentary mouthwash and spit it out in the sink, ready to see what was awaiting me upstairs.

Three men were sitting at a bar, all wearing robes identical to mine. Scott was sitting on a couch, drink in hand, with his legs tightly crossed. Young Chinese women were on each side of him, giggling continuously as he finished a dirty joke.

"B," he said, "come over here. Join us."

I gave him his key, with my own secured around my wrist.

"You like how these two girls look, B?" he asked.

"Sure."

"Sure, he says. No, for real, B. Look at these two girls. Aren't you excited that one of them is going to rub you off this morning?"

I didn't know what to say, so I just nodded.

"You've never been to a rub-and-tug, have you, B?" Scott looked at one of the girls. "You hear that, Kim Li? My friend here has never had the pleasure. You'll take good care of him, right?"

"But, of course," Kim Li said, patting my ass with a giggle. "Pleasure."

"You know why I come here, B?" Scott asked. "Simple. I come here because love is dead. And chivalry is done. I don't believe in those ideals. They're passé. I believe in what is practical. You got me? When I woke up, I had morning wood. Did you?"

"Yeah," I replied.

"Of course, you did. So what did you do about it?"

"Nothin'," I said.

"No, not nothing. You linked up with me for a rub and a tug. That's practical. No emotions involved. No sloppy decisions. No unwanted drama. When I'm hungry, I eat. When I have to shit, I shit.

When I want to cum—well, today I'm over here waiting to cum. That's the game, B. This world is full of despair, if you look at it from that perspective. I choose not to see it from that angle. I plead purposeful ignorance. I do for *me*."

Scott seemed to have it all figured out. A real salesman for narcissism. He was so sure of himself. Some of what he said made sense, but I wasn't sold. Something didn't feel quite right. His belief system just seemed too easy. A world where love is dead? There's always a catch.

The two girls stood up, gently took our hands, and led us in different directions.

14

A few days passed since the rub-and-tug. Scott had me thinking about love and life. He also had me thinking about thorough hand jobs by small women with strong forearms.

With time to kill, I ended up at Bleecker Street Records. An eclectic mix of music posters and album covers were tacked and taped up all over the walls and ceiling. Boxes of vinyl cluttered the floor here and there, waiting to be catalogued. Something special about vinyl has allowed it to endure past its time. Classic is classic.

Greenwich Village locals roamed the store in their skinny jeans tapered at the ankle. European tourists wearing Pumas and brands I had never even heard of also made their way around the store. There were even a couple of old-timers checking out the jazz 45s.

As I was digging through a pile of records, I accidentally bumped into someone next to me.

"Watch where you're goin', boss," I said before even turning my head to see who it was. Looking around, I saw a young woman crouched down, picking up a handful of records that were sprawled all over the floor.

"Excuse me?" she said, looking up. "What the hell do you mean, 'Watch where you're goin', boss?' I'm not your *boss*. Am I? And I was standing right here for, like, five minutes before you came along, so I'm pretty sure *you* bumped into *me*."

"Pardon me. It's just that I'm a dick sometimes. You know, a *real* New Yorker."

"Maybe you're just a real *dick*." She chuckled.

"Damn," I said. "You nailed it on the head."

Standing up with the records in her hand, she swiped her jet-black hair away from her eyes. She was Latina, but that's all I could figure out so far. I wanted to know more.

"Just make sure you watch where you're going next time," she said. "You might hurt someone."

"Sorry," was all I could muster.

She reached over and grabbed one more record. Then she headed up the stairs to pay. I followed her.

The cashier on the main floor had a black-and-pink Mohawk and primitive tattoos that covered most of her visible skin, including her face.

"I think you're buying my record," I said.

"I don't think so," the young woman said, taking her change and heading for the door.

I followed. "Yeah. They had it on hold for me, but they must have messed up or something, because now you got it somehow."

She cracked a perfect smile. "I've been goin' to this spot for years. I know they don't put records on hold when it's the only one they have in stock. That's why it was still on the shelf. Any other stories for me?"

I laughed somewhat uneasily. "Let's start again. My name is Byron. Some call me B. What about you?"

"Cecilia."

"Wow. That's a beautiful name. Sa-see-lee-yah. It just rolls off the tongue. Sa-see-lee-yah. Great name for a song."

Cecilia tried not to laugh, covering her stunning smile with her hand as if embarrassed that she found me humorous.

I looked her up and down. She was wearing a summery yellow dress with swirling shades of green. It only covered one of her shoulders and came down slightly lower on her left side. Bold, but she made it work.

"That's a pretty dress you got on." I couldn't resist complimenting her.

"Thanks. I made it myself."

"Bullshit," I said.

"Um, yeah, I did. That's what I do. Or wanna do, I should say."

"I'm no fashion expert, but I like what you do. I can tell you got style. Talent."

"I got some," Cecilia replied humbly.

"So, what's it gonna take for me to get that record from you?"

"I'll tell ya what. Take me out to dinner, and I'll *think* about giving it up."

"How about a recording session instead?" I asked.

"A recording session?"

"Yeah. C'mon, I gotta see a friend over at this studio in Vinegar Hill. You're not scared of Brooklyn, are ya?"

"I live and work in Red Hook."

"So ya know Brooklyn. You like good music, right?"

"You're joking?" Cecilia waved the bag of records she had just purchased.

"Just checkin'. So we got a deal?"

"Umm, we'll see about that."

Together we jumped on the F train and got off at York Street across the water. We headed up a couple flights of stairs, a long ramp, and then more stairs to reach the exit.

The evening was just arriving, leaving an uncomfortably warm Brooklyn night. I could smell the fermenting Tuesday trash set out for pickup. We walked under the Brooklyn Bridge toward the studio. When I rang the buzzer in front of the building, the door unlocked and we headed down a stairwell.

"Where the hell are you taking me?" Cecilia asked.

"Oh, you worried?" By now I was carrying her bag of records. "I can call you a car if ya want."

"Worried? Nah," she said. "But if I was, I got this." She pulled out a Taser.

"Damn, girl. Aren't those illegal?"

"So is rape," she replied, putting it back in her purse. "How did your friends end up with a space down here anyway? It smells kinda moldy."

"The dude who actually runs the studio is friends with the owner of this building. So he was allowed to use this space down here for free. You can't beat a deal like that, right?"

"I suppose. Just keep goin'."

We ventured two more flights, twisting down the cement staircase. When we reached the basement, I led us down a hallway lit by a solitary bulb. Past the boiler room was a steel door with black stenciling that read:

PUFF TUFF STUDIOS

I knocked.

As soon as the door opened, I heard music blasting and smelled chronic in the air. Very promising.

"What up, homie?" asked Primo, dapping me up. "And who's this gorgeous thing to your left?"

"Cecilia," she answered for herself.

"How ya doin', Cecilia?" Primo said, softly kissing her hand. "Um, if you'll excuse us for a second, I need to borrow B."

"Yeah," I added. "Can you just wait in that room over there? I'll be right back."

"Sure," said Cecilia.

I followed Primo into a room across the hall and closed the door.

"Listen," he said, "ya gotta call your man tonight. PM's in the other room, and he told me that he needs a P by this weekend, okay?"

"I got ya. I'll call when I get back home."

"But don't slack, aight?"

"I got ya, my brother."

"So let's talk some *real* business," Primo said, pouring a bump of coke onto the back of his hand. "Who's this bird you brought over? She's smokin' hot. How'd you hook *that* up?"

"Ya know," I said, being as cocky as possible. "She just likes what she sees."

"Get the fuck outta here with that, man," Primo said. "You want any of this blow?"

"Not now. I don't wanna get geeked up in front of the girl."

"Your loss," Primo said, sniffing down one last bump.

When we walked into the hazy room across the hall, DJ PM was talking to Cecilia and a couple of thugged-out rappers.

"All I know," PM was saying, while sitting in front of a giant mixing board, "is that I showed *him* the repercussions of pullin' that shady shit. I'm tellin' ya, man, I got, like, a sixth sense for that shit. Ain't *no one* robbin' me. Especially not no young YOLO bitch-boy still wet behind the ears." He took a pull off a blunt.

"You still talkin' about that kid with the pizza breath?" I said. "He must've had you feelin' some type of way."

"Yeah."

"*I* know what it's like to be a young punk," Primo said, smirking.

"Me too," I said, exhaling smoke.

"Yo, B," PM said. "You remember Staten Island's finest, Trü Blak and his boy, Money Payola?"

"How could I forget?" I said.

The two just eerily nodded at me from a bench they were sitting on.

"Seriously, though," PM said, "These kids today be buggin'. And I swear they keep getting younger and younger with the bullshit. Chasin' that paper. That's all they doin'—all they talk about. No heart or loyalty anymore. Not enough substance."

"Cash rules everything around us," Primo said, puffing away. "It's gonna get worse before it gets better, too. We fuckin' breed greed. Fast cash. Get-rich-quick schemes. Our priorities are all outta whack."

Cecilia nodded. "I know what you mean. Imagine if we just switched the budgets for the military and education."

"Yeah, that ain't happenin' in *our* lifetime, honey," Primo said. He put out the blunt in an ashtray. "Nah. We're Americans—doomed to be dimwitted and violent."

"*I* don't think we're doomed," Cecilia said. "There's a path for the good for all."

"Confucius?" I asked.

"The Beastie Boys," she replied.

Turning to one of the thugs on the bench, PM said, "Yo, Trü, let's lay down this verse already, my nigga."

I walked over to the mixing board next to PM, who turned up the fader until the beat was deafening. The deep bass pushed through my whole body. The melody was exotic, with blaring horns that wove in and out. All our heads involuntarily bobbed up and down to the pressing drum loop. This was a good sign.

"Put my voice up louder!" the confident MC shouted from the vocal booth, while headphones blasted in his ears. "Check one-two! One-two one-two! Word up! That's perfect!" He gave a thumbs-up through the soundproofed window and began to attack the track:

> *Yeah, basically all my life I've been livin' rough.*
> *But I've been through too much for me to start givin' up.*
> *At this point, it's nothin', I'm kinda used to it.*
> *The game brings me money, so I gotta stay true to it.*
> *I do it from the heart. I do it twenty-four-seven.*
> *Sacrificin'. Goin' to hell, so my fam can go to heaven.*
> *I guess it's just the way that it's supposed to be.*
> *I'm involved with the streets, and I'm focused, G.*
> *The cops never hesitate to do an illegal search.*
> *So now I got mami helpin' me do my dirty work.*
> *It's survival. Ya know, I'm never gonna fall.*
> *It's also strategy. I know I told you this before.*
> *So if it's gonna rain, then fuck it, let it pour.*
> *'Cause when I bring it, ya know, I bring a fuckin' storm.*
> *I gotta get this paper. I ain't got the patience.*
> *I'm findin' myself, every day, face-to-face with Satan.*

Trü Blak got his verse down in one take, adding another key ingredient to the witch's brew. The sign of a skilled lyricist.

After smoking a few more blunts, Cecilia and I looked at each other in a way that meant it was time to leave. We both complimented Trü and PM on their new track, and were just about to take off when Primo called out, "Stay outta trouble, lovebirds!"

When we got down to the York Street platform, the stagnant air waiting for us was suffocating. I looked forward to sitting in the cool air-conditioned train.

The station only housed one line — the F. One track went back to Manhattan, while the other led deeper into Brooklyn.

"I had a great time," said Cecilia, holding her bag of records. "Your friends are pretty cool."

"Thanks. So, what ya doin' now?"

Cecilia laughed as she looked at the petite and colorful Swatch that matched her self-designed dress and Nike Mids. "It's almost eleven. I gotta get home. I have work tomorrow."

"Or," I suggested with a grin, "you could come home with me."

She laughed again. Her smile was perfect. Almost too perfect. The kind you get when your dentist religiously fine-tunes your childhood braces. Wait — what if she never *had* braces?

"Nah," she said, "I ain't that type of girl. But I did have fun."

We were silent for a minute. A light appeared deep in the tunnel. Her train was coming.

"So," I said awkwardly.

"So, you gonna ask for my number, or what?"

The train screeched against the tracks as it rolled closer to the station.

"Give me your phone!" she hollered over the clamor.

I pulled out my iPhone and handed it over. The Brooklyn-bound train rushed in, pushing a hot blast of wind past us. Cecilia typed in her number, handed me the phone, and jumped on the train just before the doors slammed shut.

I mouthed, "You owe me that Sade album," as the F pulled away.

She mouthed back, "You owe me dinner!"

15

"So, is this yer Halloween getup?" Franky Golden asked, carefully eying the man in front of him. "I know dat shit is in a few days, but you didn't have to dress up already."

"Stop that, Franky. Behave," the round man said. He was wearing a black suit, black loafers, and a white button-down shirt, making him look like an oversized penguin.

"Just kiddin'," said Franky. "How ya doin', my favorite Jew? Shit, I don't befriend too many Jews, now dat I think about it. But you're still my favorite, nonetheless, Zev."

"I'm fine. How are you, Franky? I haven't seen you in a particularly long time. You found another jeweler, huh? Oy, I hope not."

Zev's curly brown hair was mostly covered with a black yarmulke. Long payos hung down in front of each ear. His wire glasses seemed too small for his pale, pudgy face. Taking them off, he wiped them carefully with his white prayer shawl.

"Of course not," said Franky. "You know you're the chosen people, right? Well, you're *my* fuckin' chosen one."

"Very funny," Zev said. "Who is this you brought with you?"

"This is Primo. And say hello to my buddy B. He's the guy I been tellin' ya about."

"Nice to meet you both. *Shalom*."

"Thanks," I replied, standing on the opposite side of a glass table.

We were in the Diamond District at 47th and Fifth. The enormous store consisted of two floors. The main level was fully open and airy, with display cases of different shapes and sizes. Precious stones and metals glistened in each case. Two C-shaped display tables formed a circle in the center of the room. Zev's co-workers were scattered about the floor, cutting deals.

"Come up to my office, gentlemen," Zev said, leading the way upstairs. His broad frame waddled from side to side, just like a penguin.

"Hey," Franky said as we walked up the stairs, "look at the piece of ass down there in the blue skirt. Mmm, mmm." He licked his lips. "She could give me her sales pitch *any* day. Hey, B, a woman like dat will suck the tip of your *piche* and convince you to buy twenty-five karats, for Christ's sake. Right, Zev? Is she one of yer top closas? I bet she's good for customas on the fence."

Zev rolled his eyes. "Franky, that's my cousin Sarah. She does light office work for us, like checking e-mails and faxes. And getting lunches. Today was kosher hot dog day at the office."

"I got a hot dog she can eat," said Franky. "A foot long. Right, B?"

I rolled my eyes. Only Golden could be so crude, but I couldn't help laughing a little inside.

Framed family pictures were scattered about Zev's cramped office. The largest ones hung on the wall next to his gemologist diploma and the brass mezuzah nailed to the doorframe. More pictures stood on his bookshelf and were arranged on his desk, along with what looked like some kind of religious book.

We all sat. Just as the Jew was about to speak, a voice from the hallway interrupted him.

"Zev?" called the voice. "Zev?"

"Father, I'm in my office."

A man walked in, dressed like Zev, but with a long silver beard. The curls on the side of his head were also silver. He looked just like I would imagine Moses looked right about the time the big G-O-D denied the man access to the Holy Land.

"Zev, I'm leaving. Remember, when you lock up, make sure you put the alarm on."

"Of course. You always remind me of that. Don't you think I remember by now?" He said this lovingly.

"Oh, I think you remember. But I also know sometimes you forget," said the man with the frizzy beard. "Aren't you going to introduce me to your clients?"

"Of course. Franky, B, Primo, this is Eli. He founded the store over forty years ago."

Primo and I nodded to the elder. Franky just sat there.

The old man recalled, "Before the Holocaust, my father, Tobias, was a jeweler in Belgium. We hid in the attic of a gentile my parents had befriended. I was only seven. We hid up there for over a year! I promised myself that if I made it out alive, I would follow in my father's footsteps."

"And here we all are," Zev said, trying to wrap up the story he had clearly heard a million times before.

"And here we all are. Alright, I'm leaving. Take care. And take the baklava and seven-layer cake that your mother left for you in my office. You know how she likes to spoil her grandchildren."

"No problem. Goodnight."

Eli walked out gingerly, favoring his right leg over his left. He looked as though he needed a cane but was probably too stubborn to use one.

"So, Franky," said Zev, "besides your perverted comments about my cousin, you've been pretty quiet since you got here. Let's see what you got for me."

Franky grabbed a paper bag from his leather jacket, and emptied the contents onto Zev's desk. A variety of chains and bracelets tumbled out, as well as a couple of class rings.

"Zev, what do you do with this jewelry?" I asked. "None of that stuff has diamonds in it."

"Gold prices are so high, we melt it all down and make bars," Zev said, sifting slowly through the pieces, examining each one with care. After a few minutes, he put the last chain down and sat back in his chair. After rubbing both of his eyes and again cleaning his glasses with the bottom of the white shawl wrapped around his neck, he said, "I can give you six hundred for all of it, Franky. Sound good?"

"Sounds good to me. Just throw in a blowjob from yer cousin, and we'll call it a deal," Franky said with no shame.

I lowered my head in embarrassment.

"I don't think that's going to happen. But I can give you a hug. I think you need one," Zev offered.

"Nah, I just need six hundred clams so I can get a blowjob." Franky chuckled to himself. "Or maybe a few of 'em if I'm lucky." He laughed louder while jabbing Primo in the ribs with his elbow. "Primo knows what I'm talkin' about. Right?"

Primo smiled uncomfortably. "Don't get me involved in your crazy antics, Franky. You're on your own with that one."

"Yeah, kid," Franky said. "I guess I'm in a class all by myself, right? But you ain't no Saint Stephen, neither. Don't forget—I know all."

Zev excused himself from the room.

"Speakin' of which," Franky added, "Primo, what's dis I hear about you hangin' around Javier Fuentes?"

"Javier Fuentes?" I said. "That's one hairy scumbag. All that degenerate wants to do is smoke crack."

"He ain't that bad," Primo said.

"He ain't that bad?" repeated Franky. "Please. Dat dude's a sack of shit in a dumpster waitin' to get picked up."

"None of us are perfect," Primo said. "We all got flaws, aight? Some more than others."

"He's a lowlife," I said.

"Oh, so *we're* better?" Primo said cynically. "What are *we* contributin' to the world? To our city? The nation? We ain't no better than the next jerk when it comes down to it. Includin' Javier. We're all just termites destroyin' this planet a day at a time. Who are we to judge?"

"I guess," I said doubtfully.

"Besides, B," Primo said, "some people would think *your* values are fucked up. Ya ever think of that? No job. Smokin' your goddamn life away." He laughed.

"In all seriousness, though, Primo," said Franky, "watch out with dat orangutan up in the Chelsea Hotel. He's trouble."

Zev walked back in, slapped his hands together, and rubbed them vigorously. "Well," he said, "everyone's left for the evening, and we're all locked up. So, B, do you have anything we can try?"

"Of course, he does," Franky said. "You think it's his first rodeo? B is like the Prime Minista of Burnin' Sinista. Where can we light one up?"

"The storage room. C'mon. I'll lead the way."

Zev waddled down the stairs, leading us into a room filled mainly with empty boxes and unused display cases. Some unfamiliar jeweler supplies and tools sat on industrial metal shelving units propped against the wall.

"So this is where yer cousin would be performin' some fellatio, huh?"

"Franky," I said, shaking my head, "you were born without a hint of couth."

"I may be uncouth, B, but I think manners is overrated anyway."

We stood near a window in the corner and smoked a spliff I had just rolled. Since I was trying to make a good first impression with the Jew, the spliff was a blend of three different strains—Snow Cap, Cinderella, and Blue Cheese. Technically, I didn't blend them, though. I laid them in the rolling paper one after the other. I could taste the different flavors as one ended and the next one began.

"Was that the Torah on your desk?" I asked Zev.

"No," he answered, choking on herb smoke. When he caught his breath, he added, "It's an English translation of the Talmud."

"What the hell is a tal-mood?" asked Franky.

"It basically breaks down Jewish laws and morals," Zev explained.

"So do you believe in god?" I asked. "Do you think he's mad that you're smokin' weed? Sinnin' and shit?" I grinned. "He can't be down with you secretly smokin' in your pop's storage room. Doesn't sound godly to me."

"I *am* a believer, but I think god makes pot, the same way he makes other plants and animals. They all serve their purpose. If *elohim* did not want me to smoke marijuana, then I would not. After all, where in the Ten Commandments does it say, 'Thou shalt not smoke sensimilla'? I don't feel his disapproval, so I get high. Besides, my eyes hurt, and marijuana seems to give me relief. Don't you believe in god, B?"

"How could there be a god that would let children die?" I asked. "Anytime I've tried to believe, let's just say I couldn't get past that question. I just think the world's too fucked up for there to be an all-powerful man in the sky watchin' over us. Please."

Visions of Willis ran through my mind. His eyes. I could see them. Not foggy, washed-out visions, but crystal-clear snapshots. His young irises were some of Mother Nature's most sublime artwork. A green base with flecks of gold layered on top, resembling a perfect autumn day. Just like today.

"It sounds like you say that from experience?" Zev asked with genuine concern.

"B's lil' bro passed away a few months ago," Primo said.

"He was a cute kid," Franky added.

"I'm sorry to hear that," Zev said. "You have to believe that it's part of the master plan, though. The *lord's* plan."

"Do I? A plan to murder an innocent kid? Nah, I don't believe that shit. You know what he died from? A genetic mutation. Childhood leukemia. There's no master plan. Shit just happens."

"When you look deep inside," asked Zev, "you don't feel his power and affection?"

"When I look deep inside?" I puffed what was left of the joint, which was now on its third and final strain. "I don't know what I feel deep down these days."

"All I know, boys," said Franky, "all I know is, whatevah the fuck is deep inside me right now, it's tellin' me dat I'm pretty fuckin' hungry. It's sayin', 'Feed me, feed me!' Anybody up for some halal?"

"Nah," I said. "Me and Primo gotta be somewhere."

16

"You see these?" Chilly asked.

Primo and I shook our heads as we sat in his living room.

"These are from a tiger shark." He ran his thumb ever so gently across the tips of the teeth. "This baby is called a *leiomano*. It's from the seventeen hundreds."

He held the weapon up to the antique floor lamp. The blade and handle were about a foot and a half long, carved from one continuous piece of wood. The blade was wide and flat like an oversized spear tip. A row of shark teeth studded the perimeter, all pointing in the same direction.

"And all you would have to do is one of these across the neck, like *this*." Chilly sliced the weapon through an imaginary foe in front of him. "Or you could get a guy across the gut or the groin. Either way, they're done. You see this?" He stuck the weapon out toward me. "See how the teeth are slightly off-center from each other? It really rips through you. This is what they designed chainsaws after. The teeth are tied on with dried cat intestines."

"Wow." I took the *leiomano* from him.

Chilly pointed to the far wall. "See, that's another one. They're both koa wood and shark teeth, but the one on the wall is called a *la'au palau*. See how it's shaped more like a knife? Besides that, they're basically used the same way. The one you're holding is worth much more, though, so I keep it locked up. I pulled out a couple treats so you could check 'em out."

"Where are these from?" I asked, staring down at the razor-sharp teeth.

"Are they Hawaiian?" Primo asked.

"They're Fijian. Both of them."

"Pretty amazin'," Primo said.

"Light that thing up already," said Chilly.

The marble coffee table in front of me was littered with stems and bits of pot leaf that had been pulled off high-quality bud. Two ashtrays were also on the square table. One was filled to the brim with pot ash. The other had recently been emptied and had a massive joint resting in it. I picked up the jay and lit it.

"I like your spot, Chilly. It's pretty dope," Primo said.

"Thanks. I've lived here, on and off, for over thirty-two years."

"What do you mean?" Primo asked.

"He means he owns the whole brownstone," I said. "Sometimes he lives here and sometimes he rents it out."

"Yeah." Chilly grabbed the joint from me. "And I usually rent out the top three floors. The money I make off that pays for my spot in Kauai."

"That works," Primo said, nodding.

"Yeah," Chilly said. "I got a real estate license and started selling and buying some small properties in the Seventies. Shit was cheap in general. The market boomed, and I sort of rode the wave." He passed the joint to Primo.

"So how the hell did you start doin' the treasure hunting?" Primo asked.

"It was a dream, I guess. So I made it a goal. I forged ahead. Learned the ins and outs. The Ps and the Qs. I became proficient at scuba diving and happened to know some people that were in the business. The rest is history. It all came to me kinda organically, if you know what I mean."

Chilly had plenty of money and seemed to have a real understanding of what's important. A true free soul who found a way to win the game—diving for treasure in the Mediterranean one day and leisurely smoking a Cuban in front of his brownstone the next. A local who made it out and back. I respect that.

His apartment was cluttered with all kinds of souvenirs from around the globe. Stunning African paintings of jungle animals and landscapes hung from the walls next to exotic and collectible weaponry. His living room was jam-packed with carved rock sculptures, a pair of ebony walking sticks, spear tips, ancient clay pottery, and many other knickknacks and treasures.

"What's that over there?" Primo asked, pointing to a thin sword resting on a brick mantel.

"That's not even for combat," Chilly said as he took the joint from Primo. "That's an accessory for a Freemason's uniform. It's just for show. Forget that one. But check *this* out."

He handed me a footlong dagger in an engraved silver sheath with a thin leather strap attached. The sheath had raised diamond patterns with a gold bead set in the center of each one. The tip of the dagger and sheath curved at almost a 90-degree angle. The handle was made of ivory and had silver plating at the end to match the sheath. I admired the precision and careful craftsmanship. After a moment, I passed the dagger back to Chilly as he passed me the joint.

"It looks like it's from *Aladdin*," Primo said.

"That's fairly accurate," Chilly replied. "It's Moroccan." He threw the strap over his left shoulder and adjusted the dagger on his right side. "This was part of Yves Saint Laurent's private collection. I love this bad boy. Just don't ask me how I got it." He swiftly pulled it out of the sheath, and once again sliced the invisible enemy in front of him. "Just like that. Or you can use the butt end. You could really whack someone good with this." He put the dagger back in its cover. Handing me another one, he said, "That's a Japanese *tanto*. It was made for either samurais or ninjas. Look at that blade—straight, narrow, and double-edged. Not flashy. Very tastefully done. And efficient. Feel how light that is? Truly extraordinary."

"When is this from?" I asked.

"It was hand-forged in the sixteenth century. I don't think it was ever used in battle. That's why it's in such mint condition."

I looked at my reflection on the thin blade.

"How many knives and swords do you own?" Primo asked.

"A fuckin' lot," Chilly said. "Too many. I'm a collector. I found my first knife on the beach when I was six and have been hooked ever since. Eventually, I expanded my collection to swords and, ya know, anything that slices and severs, pretty much."

We all laughed.

"Don't ask me why," Chilly added. "I'm pretty much a peaceful guy. Just don't take advantage of me. You know what I mean, B?" He handed me the joint.

"Yeah." I blew smoke out my nose and passed the Japanese dagger to Primo so he could get a better look.

"This is bad," Primo said. "Real bad. I need one of these."

"Ain't gonna find one quite like that too easily," Chilly said. "You can always get a knockoff, though. B, bet you never seen anything like that, have ya?"

"Huh?" I asked. The weed had me deep in thought.

Chilly looked at me with concern. "Hey, B, you okay? You seem like somethin's on your mind. I can tell when you go into that mode. Tell Uncle Chilly what's on your mind over there."

"Just been havin' a lot of crazy thoughts lately, ya know?" I was having trouble keeping my eyes open.

"Like what?" Primo asked.

"Like what the fuck are we here for?" I said. "And what the fuck am I doin' with my life? I used to not really give a shit about that stuff."

"We were young," Primo said. "And reckless. Only livin' for the moment."

"I know. But now something's different," I said.

Chilly sat down next to me and began to roll another large joint. "Thinking about who you are and what you wanna be," he said. "Thinking about what you want in this world. It's normal to have thoughts like that. And it's normal to have doubts and feel uncertain about what the future holds. Me and you are thinking men, B. Minds like ours make it extremely difficult to be fully content. But that doesn't mean we shouldn't try."

"It's like ever since my baby brother died, I've been feeling different," I said. "Like something's pushing me forward, pushing me to do something more. But I don't know what. I have no college degree or even a real skill set. It's scary."

"Of course, it's scary, sweetheart," Chilly said. "Nobody ever said it wasn't, B. It's also painful and shitty. But there's another side which makes most of us wanna get up in the morning. Hope and anticipation. Ya see? Maybe a new day will bring new pleasure."

"New morning dew fed the starving grass that grew," I said.

Chilly lit up the giant cone-shaped joint with a chrome Zippo and blew a cloud of smoke into the light above us. "What's that from?"

"Something I wrote once."

"I like that," Primo said.

"Remember, B," Chilly said, "*both* of you, remember that all of this, all of this stuff that surrounds you, this society, this capitalist design we live in—it's not natural. It's largely a fraud. A fake. An illusionary facade, hiding what really matters. Don't believe them when they tell you to do things their way and in their format. Don't believe 'em! The truth is that we live on this planet to do just that— *live!* We're not here to work to the grave for someone else, doing something we don't care about. Doesn't that sound absurd to you guys when you hear it out loud?"

"Yeah," I said, taking a few puffs. The smoke in the room was getting milkier.

"A job. A wife. Two-point-two kids. A dog. A cat. A goddamn goldfish?" Chilly was getting worked up by now. "That may be right for some, but I say fuck all that, man. In my experience, you have to do what you have to do, not what other people want you to do. That's how I've always lived. My way. Like Mr. Sinatra, you know?"

"I hear that," Primo said.

"You might think that sounds selfish, huh, B?" Chilly took the spliff. "It ain't selfish. And to give in to this *Matrix*-like system, well that's cowardly. Don't ya see?"

"That makes sense," I said, still not convinced.

"Look, B. In the end, you have to answer to your own conscience. Is yours clear?"

"I'm not really sure. I don't know."

"You *need* to know. Both of you. And the sooner you do, the sooner you'll actually be able to sleep peacefully when you go to bed. I sleep like a log." Chilly said this with a wink. "B, you're a good kid. You're a bright kid. Trust me, in the end you're gonna be alright. I promise. Do something you enjoy. That keeps you young. And eventually you'll be where you're supposed to be." He took another drag and put out the roach. "So what do you guys have for me?"

I reached into my black book bag and pulled out a sealed package. "This," I said. "It's right up your alley, too. Elvis."

"The King?"

"You know it," Primo said.

Chilly cut the bag of Elvis open with the Japanese dagger and took a whiff.

"Oh, yeah! Fit for a king! No question! How much for the whole QP?"

"Twenty-one hundred," I said.

"Perfect. I'm going to Tonga in about a week and a half for another expedition, so that should last me just long enough."

"Damn!" Primo said. "You might actually smoke more than us."

We laughed.

"Let me grab some cash," Chilly said. "I gotta put these treasures away anyway."

He picked up the Moroccan dagger, the samurai *tanto*, and the Fijian battle gear and headed downstairs.

17

"Look at this idiot," Primo said, nodding at the TV. "Hope? What hope has he given? He's no different than the rest. Maybe he gets a D minus instead of an F."

"I think he's pretty honest sometimes," I said as I rolled a Vanilla Dutch Master. "At least he's way better than Bush was."

Primo was sitting at my desk, weighing out some weed. "Fuckin' Bush. How *that* chimp won, I'll never understand."

"You didn't vote, Primo, so you can't say squat."

With the help of a crème brûlée torch, Primo smoked a dab of oil from a small glass bubbler. After exhaling, he said, "Yeah, and I never will! Not for these liars. Besides, that shit's fixed anyway, aight?"

"Here we go with the conspiracy theories again." I rolled my eyes as I lit up the Dutch.

"You know it's true. Big Brother. CIA coups. Nine-Eleven. This is a shady fuckin' country that was built on deceit."

"Even so, we're lucky that we live here. It could be worse."

"We ain't on top anymore, B. You know we're only livin' off loans from other countries, right? China? The American Dream's in a dirty pine box buried under a giant pile of shit."

"That's quite a visual," I said.

"Tell me I'm lyin'! We sabotaged ourselves. Eatin' ourselves from the inside out. Fuckin' cannibalism! That's why this country's goin' to hell in a handbasket. The first undeveloping nation."

He said all this as he labeled the bags he had weighed.

"You're right. We're fucked." I blew out smoke and passed him the blunt of Headband.

"I feel bad for the newbies," Primo said. "They're gonna have it worse than us. I wouldn't wanna be a kid right now. The future looks bleak."

"Oh, shit," I said. "That reminds me. I almost forgot. We gotta meet Ajani and Cecilia by Mamoun's. They're probably there already."

Packing his goods into a white shopping bag, Primo said, "I'm leavin' this here till tomorrow." Then he waved an orange script bottle filled with Percocets. "You want one?"

"Nah. I'm good."

Opening the lid, he popped two white pills into his mouth.

"How many of those have you eaten today?"

"This is only five."

"Five? You should chill on those, Primo. That shit is bad for your liver."

"Man, *fuck* my liver! I got pain."

"What pain?"

"Right here." He pointed to his heart.

I turned off the TV, and we headed out the door.

Cecilia and Ajani were waiting in front of Mamoun's Falafel on St. Marks.

"Look who finally decided to join us," she said.

"Sorry," I apologized, grinning sheepishly. "We got caught up for a minute."

"Of course, you did. Hi, Primo. How ya doin'?"

"Not bad." He leaned in to give her a peck on the cheek. "And what about you, lil' man?" he said to Ajani. "You good?"

"Yeah," the boy answered.

"Shall we?" Cecilia asked.

We ordered some falafel sandwiches with hummus and sat down

at the few tables set up outside. The thermometer that was stuck to the front window read 65 degrees—an unseasonably warm fall evening, perfect for eating a cheap meal under the stars.

As we were finishing, a school bus pulled up in front, painted in army-green camouflage, down to the hubcaps. Immediately after the door flung open, a crew of teens piled out. Some went into Mamoun's, and the rest went to the sushi spot across the street. I smelled patchouli oil as they rushed past me.

"Holy shit!" I said. "Yo, Primo. Look who just walked outta that thing."

"Is that Cam?" Primo asked, scratching his neck. "It is!"

The four of us walked over to the beat-up bus, which was blasting hippie music. Cam was standing in front, yawning, with his skinny arms stretched out over his head. Vitiligo had made some of his face and arms spotted pink. He was sporting a ripped Champion hoodie and some sweats that were too short for his long legs. His socks looked stained and worn.

"What's up, guys? I haven't seen you in years!"

"Hey, Cam. It's good to see ya," Primo said. "Last I heard, you got popped."

"Yup. Got run-up on by the goons in the paddy wagon one night. I had some weed, and next thing I know, they got me for child support, too. Ain't that a bitch? How the fuck am I supposed to pay what I don't even got, huh? Let that be a lesson, kid." He said this looking down at Ajani. "Don't have a baby till you're ready. And also, don't ever trust a pig in blue. By the way, who are *you*, kid?"

"This is my partner, Ajani," I said. "And this is Cecilia."

"Oh, B. She's a beautiful young thing." Cam's smile was crooked.

A short young brunette no older than sixteen walked out of the bus, wearing nothing but a cutoff tee and cotton panties with ice cream cones on them. She rubbed her eyes and looked way up at Cam.

"Go in the sushi spot, baby. You can use the bathroom there," he said.

The girl said nothing. She just turned away and walked barefoot across the street. Ajani's eyes were fixated on her ass.

"Hey," I said as I smacked the boy on his arm. "Don't worry about that yet. You're too young."

"No, I ain't!"

"Oh, you like Suzy?" Cam asked. "That's my new old lady."

"Old lady? She's, like, twenty years younger than you," I said.

"Yeah. She's a runaway. And get this—she's a virgin."

"Dear lord," Primo said. "You're gonna hurt her, Cam."

"What do you mean?" Ajani asked.

"Never mind that," Cecilia said swiftly. "We should get going. Ajani has school tomorrow, B."

"You wanna check out the bus?" asked Cam, ignoring Cecilia's comment. "We even got a hot tub in there."

"Really?" Primo asked.

"Yeah. But right now it's bein' used as a makeshift bed. We got nitrous, too! A few twenty-pounders. We're about to eat some mushrooms and suck some gas. Maybe go to Brooklyn Bowl later and see Questlove spin some records. You guys should come along. Heard Joey Badass might show up."

"I wish we could," I said, not meaning it. "But I gotta walk this young punk home." I obnoxiously rubbed the top of Ajani's head.

"I'll take a trip with ya," Primo said.

"No doubt," said Cam. "You got some bud?"

18

I WANT TO STAY AS CLOSE TO THE EDGE AS I CAN WITHOUT GOING OVER. OUT ON THE EDGE YOU SEE ALL KINDS OF THINGS YOU CAN'T SEE FROM THE CENTER.

—KURT VONNEGUT

I'VE ALWAYS BEEN ONE TO ENJOY A RUSH. UNFORTUNATELY, MANY WAYS TO ENJOY A GOOD RUSH ARE AGAINST THE LAW, AND THEREFORE MAKE ME A CRIMINAL. BUT I'VE KNOWN FROM A YOUNG AGE THAT I WASN'T THE TYPE TO GO THE STRAIGHT-AND-NARROW. I HAD OTHER PLANS, THINKING I KNEW WHAT THE HELL I WAS DOING. LOOKING BACK, I REALIZE THE AGE-OLD SAYING RINGS TRUE—IGNORANCE IS BLISS.

THE BOTTOM LINE IS: THIS IS THE LIFE I PICKED. I COULD BE SOMEONE ELSE. A PROFESSOR OR A SCRUFFY DOCK WORKER. A TYRANNICAL BOSS OR A MEEK SUBORDINATE. A WALL STREET TRADER OR A WALMART GREETER. ENDLESS WAYS TO LIVE ONE'S LIFE.

MINE IS A DIFFERENT BREED THAN MOST. I LIVE MAINLY OFF THE RADAR ON THE OUTSKIRTS. ABUSING DRUGS, SEX, LOUD MUSIC, WHATEVER

HIGHS I CAN FIND. NOT COMFORTABLE IN MY
SOBER SKIN. NOT COMFORTABLE WITH THE
SCANDALOUS SETUP AROUND ME.
    A LIFE OF WEIRD EXTREMES. SWINGING FROM
ONE TO THE OTHER CAN BE VERY DANGEROUS,
BECAUSE THERE IS NO BALANCE AND YOU CAN
EASILY LOSE CONTROL. ON THE OTHER HAND,
NEVER MOVING FAR FROM THE CENTER PRESENTS
ITS OWN DANGER—LIVING A LIFE THAT IS STAGNANT
AND OVERWHELMINGLY PREDICTA

"Freeze, motherfuckers!" yelled a man holding a sawed-off
shotgun.

He had a green-and-white ski mask with a Jets logo pulled down
over his face. His eyes scanned Chang's laundromat through two
slits in the mask.

"Everyone get down on the fuckin' ground! Take off your jewelry
and slide it all to me! That includes purses and wallets!"

He grabbed the guy closest to him by the collar and tossed him to
the floor. I quickly got down, along with a dozen others. Their faces
were trembling. A terrified woman was lying on her side, clutching
a toddler with one arm and taking off her necklace with the other.

For some reason, I wasn't afraid. When the robber was looking
the other way, I quietly slipped my notebook in my jeans by my
waist. I had been waiting in the laundromat for Chang to come back
from the pizzeria around the corner, but he had taken a while, so I
had figured I would jot down some ideas in the meantime. But this
masked man had other plans for me.

My silver money clip clanked against the white cement floor as
I slid it toward the anxious fuck with the green ski mask. I could see
Lu Chu on her knees in the back of the laundromat, distraught that
she had gotten caught away from the back office where she could
have locked the door and called the police. I just stayed silent on my
stomach.

Don't panic. Stay calm. Stay alert, I thought.

"No one try that funny shit, or they'll get it between the eyes! I ain't kiddin'! My aim is vicious! Y'all got me?!"

The robber's voice showed no doubts.

I was on my belly, looking at his sloppily cuffed jeans tucked half in and half out of his brown steel-toed Tims.

Starting at the front and making his way back, the robber scooped up his loot as fast as he could. But he only made it ten steps before a voice came from the front door.

"I would think about what you're doing, son," the voice said. "This is not the path to enlightenment or success. At best, you'll die prematurely, but as a free man."

"Who the fuck is *you*, pops? Ain't no one asked your opinion. Just get down on the fuckin' floor like everyone else before you get hurt-up quick. Don't be a hero."

"A free man if you're lucky," said the voice. "Worse, though, you die behind bars as a number. Not a person."

Chang slowly crept closer while his hypnotic voice kept the gunman's attention.

"You think you're the first person to tell me that bullshit, pops? I got bills to pay. I need that paper now! So just throw your wallet over here and get on the ground like the rest. You ain't any different, black man."

At point-blank range, he aimed his sawed-off shotgun straight at Chang.

"Son," Chang said, "you don't wanna go this route. It doesn't lead anywhere prosperous. It's a dead end."

The man stayed positioned with his finger on the trigger.

"Hey!" I called. "Can we move this along, please? I got other shit to do, ya know."

"What the fuck did you just say to me, bitch?"

The robber pointed the sawed-off in my direction.

"I said hurry up. If I'm gonna get robbed, I at least wanna get some pussy before the end of the night to make up for this shit. So let's go. Keep it movin'. My girl's waitin' at home, man."

"You stupid fuck! I should fire this shit right in your ass!"

Chang saw an opportunity. A quick kick to the kidney. A short swift chop to the neck. Chang fluidly snatched the weapon.

"You see what I'm saying, youngster?" he asked, looking down at the dazed criminal who was still trying to breathe. "You gotta get your shit together. You won't last long like this. Take off the Jets mask."

The defeated crook looked up and took off his winter cap. The intimidating man who had been barking behind a mask actually had a baby face and not a hair on his chin. That took me by surprise.

"Now," continued Chang, as he kept the sawed-off pointed right at him, "you apologize to everyone in here, you got me? Take everyone's stuff out of your pockets, put it all back on the floor, and apologize."

The boy emptied his pockets and somberly mumbled, "I'm sorry."

"You better be, you no-good piece of scum!" shouted a man getting his courage back. "They should lock you up and throw away the damn key!"

"You see, boy? That's what's gonna happen to you if you don't get your act together one of these days," Chang prophesized. Then he motioned his eyes to the front door. "And remember, I don't *ever* forget a face."

The young robber sprinted out of the laundromat as fast as lightning. Chang went to help up his wife, who was drying her eyes.

"What the hell?" said a woman, picking up her purse from the ground. "Why did you let him get away?"

"You could have stopped him," Chang said. "Any of you could have. What did you want, huh? Did you want me to shoot him in the back as he ran away? No, I don't think so. I don't need that on my conscience. Shooting another black man? No, thank you."

No one said anything. Eventually, a few of the customers dialed 911 on their cell phones. Others gathered their laundry, reclaimed their briefly stolen possessions, and scurried out the door.

I grabbed my money clip from the ground and stared at Chang uneasily.

He placed his hand on my shoulder. "You look like you wanna ask me something."

"Why did you let that scumbag go? I don't get it."

"The Tao has a funny way of working these things out, B. Lao Tzu said that those who seek will find, those who reform will be forgiven, the good will be rewarded, and… the thief who is cunning will escape." Chang said these last words with a grin. "That boy wasn't cunning at all now, was he? He needed help escaping so that he could hopefully reform and then be forgiven. You and I, we're good, so we'll be rewarded. Forgiveness is good for the spirit. You got me?"

"Yeah," I answered, even though I was completely unsure of what Chang meant. He had lost me, but he seemed to sense this.

"Let me put it this way, Byron. That young man is a scumbag today, a positive force tomorrow. If not, you know where he'll end up."

I could hear the cop cars pulling up in front with their sirens blaring.

"But one thing's for sure," Chang added. "He ain't *never* gonna try *me* again. Now get outta here before these guys come inside. Don't worry, I don't know you."

I darted to the rear into Chang's apartment and managed to slip out the back just as the cops were entering the front.

19

"You look beautiful," I said to Cecilia.

She always does, so I try to tell her as often as I can.

She squeezed my hand. "Why, thank you, my sexy man."

When we walked out of Santos Party House, DJ PM had just finished spinning records. Cecilia and I had danced all night, rubbing all over each other. My moves were amateurish, but at least I had my drink and my two-step.

It was a little after four in the morning, and dawn was on its way. Winter was coming any day now, and the still air was crisp and refreshing. We buttoned up our coats and walked northeast on Lafayette toward my apartment.

"Amazing, huh? Barely anyone out here," I said. "Millions of people runnin' around these streets. Not now. Listen to how quiet is. How much space we have. Pretty cool."

"I'm not usually awake at this hour," Cecilia said, "let alone outside. But, yeah, I can appreciate what you're saying." She held my hand. "It does feel kind of romantic. I mean, with just the two of us out here."

"There's that pack of bums sleepin' right over there, too" I said, pointing to the left.

She laughed as we kept walking.

Soon we turned the corner onto Bond Street. It was even more desolate. Sitting down on one of the stoops that wasn't gated off, I lit a half-smoked joint.

"You're right," Cecilia said. "This feels nice. I would never hang out here alone. But with you—I like it."

"Yeah, this city never sleeps, but it definitely takes a nap." I passed the joint to Cecilia, who smoked silently while I wrapped my arm around her for warmth.

"Just look at that full moon, Byron. It's so big and bright. Incredible, right?"

"Oh, no. I think I... I... I feel my skin itching. What's happening?!" I looked at my arms, which curled up toward me.

"What's the matter, B? Are you okay? Too much tequila?"

"I'm not sure. I... I... I'm becoming part werewolf!" I looked up to the moon above. "Owwwoooooooo! Oww-oww-owwwooooooooo!"

Cecilia looked at me the way she often did—with eyebrows raised. "You're a weirdo, yo."

"So what?"

"What happened to quiet and peaceful?" she asked.

"Fuck it. Sometimes it's good to disturb the peace. Shake things up a bit." I took a hit. "You ever howl at the moon at four-thirty in the morning?"

"No."

"Sooo?"

She smiled. Then she cupped her hands around her lips and started howling.

As I smoked what was left of the jay, admiring the attractive she-wolf in front of me, a couple of rats seemed to be playing with each other as they circled metal garbage cans ready for pickup.

"C'mon, troublemaker," I said. "We better make moves before someone comes out to shut us up."

We got to my apartment fifteen minutes later. Soon after, Sade was spinning on the turntable, and Cecilia was spinning on top of me. Her hair hung down, still drying from the quick shower she had just taken. She was wearing a skimpy white nightie that stopped high up on her thighs. Her body smelled of lavender. The sweet haze from the joint I had lit while she showered still lingered above us. Cinnamon-scented candles were glowing on the mantel. It was an aromatherapy session.

When I woke up a few hours later and felt beside me, Cecilia wasn't there. Just a pillow. The room was flooded with morning light. I sat up and squinted. Cecilia was sitting at the foot of the bed, still in the white lace nightie.

"What are you doin' down there?" I asked.

The morning rays pierced through the window, reflecting off her back. She turned to me with a sober stare, holding up a few sheets of loose-leaf paper. "You write?"

"Yeah. And I can read, too."

"I'm serious, Byron. You write? Like for *real*?"

"I mean, some. I wouldn't say for real."

"You write? Why wouldn't you tell me that? How long have we been going out now? Almost four months. How could you not tell me something like that?"

"I don't know. I guess I keep that info close to the vest."

"I can see that. If I hadn't tripped on your sneaker on my way back from the bathroom and knocked over this pile of clothes, I *still* wouldn't have seen all this."

She pointed down to the stack of papers, now strewn across the floor, unhidden. I had forgotten to put the stack back in my closet after I read through it yesterday. I blame the weed.

"You would've just kept me in the dark?" she continued. "Till when? That pile is your thoughts and dreams, and you didn't want to share that with me?"

"Of course, I do. I did. It's not that. It's—"

"It's *what*?"

"I guess it's just that I'm afraid," I answered honestly.

"Afraid of what?"

"Failure. Failing the art. Expressing my feelings in a shitty and clichéd way instead of the way it's supposed to be done. How could I just jump in like I'm part of that scene? A writer. An author. An artist. People would think, *Look at this guy. He doesn't belong at this table. This is the grown-up table. Go sit over there with the kiddies at the kiddie table."*

I reached over to my nightstand and grabbed a lighter and a roach of the Raspberry Haze spliff we had shared five hours earlier, and lit up.

"From what I'm reading," she said, sliding next to me on the bed, "you have talent. I'm named after Cecília Benevides de Carvalho Meireles. Do you know who that is?" She was speaking softly. Her slight accent was so sexy.

I shook my head.

After taking a hit on the roach, she said, "Cecília Meireles is one of Brazil's most famous poets. She was also a journalist and teacher. You think she had it easy?"

I shrugged my shoulders.

"No," Cecilia replied, as she started to get dressed. "Her papa and siblings died before she was born, and her mama died when she was three. That was just the start. Artists are meant to suffer. That's how they're able to see things clearly and truly appreciate the beauty and awe of it all."

I thought to myself, *The yin and the yang.*

"Byron, you have to get over your fears. Fears are prisons to be freed from."

"That is truly insightful. Can I steal that quote for a story I'm writing?"

"You're a real dick. You can't ever be serious, can you?" She was smiling as she said this. "You can't worry about what other people think, B. You have one life to live. Take hold of it. Don't let your life just dictate itself."

She sounded a lot like my mother, but I wouldn't dare tell her. I could catch a slap for that.

"Have you ever had anything published at all or talked to anyone in the business?" she asked.

Penny's face came to mind. Spectacles on the tip of her nose. A know-it-all New York attitude in her smirk.

"I've never had anything published. I mean, besides in my grade school yearbook and shit. And a few things online." I paused, then added, "I met a woman in the industry right before I met you. Her name's Penny."

"What did she say to you?"

"She said I should keep in touch with her."

"Have you?"

"No."

"Baby, why not? Didn't you like her? Was she pretentious?"

"No. Actually, I really liked her from that one time we met. I guess I just let it go by the wayside. I don't really have a good excuse, ya know?"

"It's your fears that are holding you back, B."

I said nothing. The truth stung.

"I want to meet Penny," Cecilia said, pulling her hair back into a ponytail. She leaned in toward the mirror, sticking out her lovely ass, and picked at her perfect teeth with her pinky nail. "Let's invite her out to dinner."

"Nah. Fuck it."

"Why, Byron?"

"I just don't want to."

"Because you're scared!"

"Stop with that shit, alright!" I snapped.

With that, she started to pack up her belongings.

"C'mon, Cecilia. Are you really leavin' now?"

She stopped packing. "Yes, B. I'm leaving now. And I'm leaving for good. This doesn't work for me. You're scared to go for it, Byron. You have to take the plunge."

"Will you stop being over the top, please? Just come back to bed with me for a bit."

"B, I have something to tell you, too."

"What?" I asked, still under the blankets.

"I think I'm moving to Paris."

"What do you mean?"

"I'm going to Paris to apprentice under Alber Elbaz. I don't even know what that fully means, but my friend Monique is already over there working for Lanvin. She called a few days ago and told me that she had showed some of my designs to Alber himself, and he said I had promise. Can you *believe* that? Promise. Monique told me to get over there as soon as possible so I can start collaborating with them. I'm so happy. I still can't believe it when I say it out loud."

"Wow," I said, shocked. "When did you find out?"

I could tell she sensed the wariness in my voice.

"Aren't you at least a *little* happy for me?"

"Of course," I said unconvincingly. "I just… I mean… what does that mean for *us*?"

"It means we could keep in touch every day. Skype. You could send me love letters in the mail. You could come and visit, and we could walk along the Seine together. But, I just don't know, Byron. Your lifestyle is too much for me sometimes. And it hurts deep down that you kept your creativity hidden. I just think I need some space right now."

"That sounds like *too* much space," I said sadly.

"This is a once-in-a-lifetime opportunity for me, B." She had calmed down again and sat next to me on the bed. "I have to take the plunge, sweetie," she whispered.

"Don't leave me. Not now."

"Call Penny, and maybe we'll talk."

Cecilia grabbed her purse and gently kissed me on the lips before walking out the door.

20

"Nigga, I don't owe you a dime!" Pedro said.

"Look, that blow was garbage," said the thin black boy. "I want my fuckin' money back, you fat fuck."

"Who you callin' fat, you gangly bastard? Al, you're like two-dimensional," Pedro taunted. "When you turn sideways and shit, I can't even see you no more. Fuck, I'm surprised you don't just slip right through that smelly-ass sewer grate." He pointed to the grate by Al's feet.

Pedro laughed along with Ajani and Chris Parker, who were standing beside him with their hands folded. The three friends had just left Pedro's apartment, stocked with Christmas candy canes. Pedro lived only a handful of buildings away from Ajani's place in the Lillian Wald complex. They were on their way to the Mound when Al approached them.

"Yeah, please, Pedro. *You* know, and *I* know, that shit you been servin' is stepped on more than your mama's pussy."

"Oh, now we talkin' mamas?" Pedro said with a scowl.

"All three of you niggas know what I'm talkin' about!" Al shouted. "Don't play dumb!"

"You wanna quiet down, huh?" Ajani said calmly.

"Yeah, you want the whole neighborhood to know?" Chris Parker asked.

Pedro waved for the older boy to walk over to him. At five feet and ten inches, Al towered over the three boys.

"How about I give you ten bucks off your next purchase?" Pedro asked. "What do you think about that?"

"What do I think about *that*?" Al repeated. "What do I think about *that*? I think that's bullshit. *That's* what I think about that. I want all sixty bucks back."

"Where's the bag, then?" Chris Parker asked.

"Huh?"

"Yeah," agreed Pedro. "Where's the bag, nigga? If you go to fuckin' Macy's, and you want your money back, you sure as hell better have the socks you're returnin'."

"I don't got it no more."

"What do you mean, you don't got it no more?" Pedro asked.

"It's gone," Al muttered.

"Huh? I can't hear you," Pedro said. "Can you speak up a smidge?"

"It's gone, nigga! We did all the coke! That's how I know it's such shit!"

"You are fuckin' outta your mind if you think I'm givin' you a nickel back, yo. In fact, you don't get *anything* off next time. *En-nee-thing!* You know why?"

"Why?"

"Because I don't fuckin' *like* you. That's why. So get your bony ass outta here."

Al's eyes popped out in rage. He grabbed Pedro's collar, drew back, and punched him in the eye.

Ajani reached up and tried to choke the taller and stronger freshman.

Al backed away quickly and pulled out a small Swiss Army knife. "Which one of you wants some first? The fat fuck? That's who *I* want first." Al charged at Pedro, who was frozen from terror with eyes tightly shut.

Pop! Pop! Pop!

Three shots fired in the air. Chris Parker was holding a Derringer .38 Special.

Al took one look at the gun and bolted as fast as he could.

"Drop that shit in the gutter," Ajani said.

Chris Parker wiped the .38 with his jacket and dropped it down the sewer grate, all in a matter of seconds. The three started to run as fast as they could.

Police sirens were already wailing from only a few blocks away.

"We need to split up, or they'll get us all!" Ajani warned.

They each cut through the complex in different directions.

Ajani sprinted as fast as his legs would take him. When he got near his place, he saw Byron leaving the building next door.

The sirens were getting closer and closer.

21

Ajani came running up to me. I could tell by his eyes that something was wrong, and I could hear sirens a block away.

"Where you goin'?" he asked, out of breath.

"I was picking up a few of Will's things that I wanted to keep. Now I'm headed home."

"Can I come with you?" he asked, looking around nervously.

"Yeah, of course. Let's get outta here."

"Let's catch a cab," Ajani said.

We could have easily walked, but I let Ajani quickly lead me down the block to hail a yellow cab.

On the short ride to my place on Avenue C, he explained quietly what had just happened. I was disappointed, to put it mildly.

"You know what?" I said. "I don't like your partners, lil' man. And I *definitely* don't want you hustlin' powder. *Any* powders. You're only twelve, for Christ's sake. You wanna end up in goddamn juvey?"

Ajani didn't answer. He just kept his head bowed.

"Me and you are goin' on a mission real fast." I shouted to the driver, "Hey, boss, can you take us to Brooklyn, please?"

"Where to, my friend?" the Indian driver asked.

"Across the Manhattan Bridge toward downtown," I answered.

"You got it, my friend," he said, making a hard turn onto Avenue C.

I looked back at Ajani with a straight face. "You're gonna meet a good friend of mine. You think Chris Parker and Pedro are gonna help you become a real man? I don't think so. I think they're both headed to the bing. You wanna meet a real man? Real intelligence? Well, I'm gonna bring you right to the source."

I could tell the boy was wondering who this mystery man would be.

"Boss, what's up with the heat back here?" I asked the driver.

"Oh, so sorry. The heater isn't working. I have to get the darn thing fixed. So sorry, sir."

Ajani started to shiver. His hands were tucked into his sleeves.

"Here," I said, taking off my gloves. "Keep these. They shouldn't be too big on ya."

Ajani took the gloves and put them on.

"What the hell am I gonna do?" he asked desperately. "I feel like I'm trapped."

I took a deep breath. "You gotta figure a way outta here, man. I know you don't wanna be on the block your whole life, right? In the Lillian Wald complex? Hangin' with the winos and the junkies? Or servin' 'em up?"

"Hell, no. I just don't know what to do. I need help."

We were silent for a little while.

"I went to California once," I said. "Flew to L.A. to visit Norah's sister."

"What was it like?"

"Sunshine. Surfing. No winters."

"Sounds like paradise."

"We picked a pineapple from in my aunt's backyard, sliced it up, and ate it right then on the spot."

"Damn." Ajani's face lit up.

"That's just one pinprick on the map, kid. There are so many places for you to go. Wait till you're a little older and just go."

I looked out the window as we crossed the Manhattan Bridge. "How's your mom been doin' these days?"

"She drinks too much," Ajani said, frowning. "She's an alcoholic."

"I'm sorry you gotta deal with that."

"So am I." He paused. "Ya know, I hang out with Chris Parker and Pedro all day. They're cool most of the time. I swear. And we make money together, ya know? But I never told you, B—you're my best friend. You're pretty much the only person I can trust."

I didn't know what to say. But I blurted out, "I'm always gonna be there for you, Ajani. I mean that."

"Thanks."

"We just gotta keep you outta trouble. You're too young to be gettin' shoved into those paddy wagons. We ain't tryin' to have that happen. Understand?"

Ajani nodded as I looked into his dark brown eyes.

When we got out of the cab in downtown BK, he seemed less cold and more at ease. Perhaps it was the absence of police sirens. I led the way inside the laundromat, walked to the back, and knocked on the door to the office.

Lu Chu let us in. She was sweating through her white gi. I gave her a hug and introduced Ajani, who took off his new gloves to shake her hand.

"Oh, my goodaness. You such handsome boy," she told Ajani. "Let me pinch." She quickly grabbed his cheek. "Oh, I could eat you up. Dericious. Chang downstairs. Come with me, you two anjers."

We followed Lu Chu down the stairs. Chang was practicing kung fu, also sporting a white gi. His black belt was frayed but stood out proudly.

"Hey, baby boy!" Chang called. He took a couple of breaths and wiped his forehead with a towel.

The punching bag squeaked as it slowly swung to a stop.

"Me and the better half were just getting a workout before dinner." He turned to Lu Chu. "Baby doll, can you go upstairs and make a pot of matcha? I'll be up in a while."

"But, of course." The husband and wife bowed to each other, then Lu Chu turned toward us. "Goodnight, boys," she said, and happily scurried up the stairs.

"She'll beat your ass," Chang said, as serious as a heart attack, before smiling wide.

"How are you, Chang?" I asked. "I brought a visitor. He's a bit shady, though." I rubbed the top of Ajani's head. "But I got my eye on him."

"Oh, don't worry, baby boy," Chang said. "I got *both* of my eyes on him." He looked over at Ajani. "You got me, boy? I got both these ol' crow eyes on you."

Ajani stood there silent, not sure how to respond. Chang and I laughed.

"Chang, this is Ajani," I said.

"Relax, Ajani," Chang said. "I'm just messing around. It's nice to meet you."

"*I'm* not messin' around," I said seriously. "This kid's been runnin' amok lately, and I don't like it. He and his two boys—they're like three blind mice."

"Ah, I see," Chang said. "You know what happened to the three blind mice, correct?"

"No, sir."

"They got their tails cut off with a carving knife."

"That's almost what happened today," I said. "But he got away this time. Isn't that right, Ajani?"

The boy was too embarrassed to say anything.

I pulled out a white paperback from my bag. "Here," I said to Chang. "Thanks for the read. I really enjoyed it. I mean, I could relate to a bunch of it. Bruce Lee was the man."

"Indeed, he was." Chang took the book from me and in one fluid motion passed it to Ajani. "And here you go, lil' man. True wisdom for someone who needs it."

"Thanks," Ajani said, graciously accepting the book and starting to thumb through it.

"No problem. We'll teach you yet." Chang gave me a wink.

"Won't we, Byron?"

I nodded, truly hoping we would.

"I want you to ask me any questions you have as you're reading that," Chang said to Ajani.

"Actually, *I* have a question," I said. "Since we came here on a mission of enlightenment today, I was hoping you could explain a bit about the Tao. Could you?"

Chang wiped more sweat from his face with a towel and pointed to a couple of folding chairs. Ajani and I sat down.

"Let me start like this," Chang said directly, as if he had recited this speech countless times. "We are all one. No matter how individual and separate you think you are, let me tell you that you are not. We are, in fact, all interconnected. We grow from the Earth together and are made of the same atoms as the stars. The great Tao flows everywhere. The wise Lao-tzu once said:

> *The great Tao flows everywhere.*
> *All things are born from it,*
> *Yet it doesn't create them.*
> *It pours itself into its work,*
> *Yet it makes no claim.*
> *It nourishes infinite worlds,*
> *Yet it doesn't hold on to them.*
> *Since it is merged with all things*
> *And hidden in their hearts,*
> *It can be called humble.*
> *Since all things vanish into it*
> *And it alone endures,*
> *It can be called great.*
> *It isn't aware of its greatness;*
> *Thus it is truly great.*

He stroked his Fu Manchu.

"There is a balance, Ajani," he continued. "A yin and a yang. The wood and drywall that frames your house, and the emptiness inside that allows you to live freely within. The yin and the yang. Not opposites, but rather two complementary halves of the same whole. Both are to be cherished, even if it is difficult to do so. They are forever locked together. Male and female. Animal and plant. Day and night. Pleasure and pain. Love and hate. The list goes on. The point is balance. Without one, you would not truly have the other."

While looking at Ajani, I asked Chang, "What does Taoism say about violence and negative influences?"

"The *Tao Te Ching* warns us not to use violence," Chang said. "Because violence has a nasty habit of returning. Right on your doorstep. Understand, boy?"

"Yes, sir," Ajani answered.

"Good. You use violence as a last line of defense, and that's it. It serves no other positive purpose. Don't let anyone tell you differently. Steer clear of negativity, so you can be its positive counterpart. Keep your lifestyle as clean as possible. B, have *you* been steering clear of negativity? Living as clean as possible?"

"No comment," I answered. "Why don't you show Ajani some of that fancy footwork of yours?" I was trying to divert the conversation.

"Okay, baby boy," Chang said. "You're off the hook, for now. One last thing, Ajani, and that will be all for today's lesson. Understand that you are not just your physical body. Did you know that?"

"No, sir."

"It's true. You are also the extended energy, thoughts, emotions, and actions that you put out to the universe. Always remember that. You'll realize how extensive and immense your whole being actually is. Imagine what good you can do with such a powerful commodity."

"Yes, sir," the boy said.

"I'm talking to you, too, B."

"Yes, sir," I said with a nod.

"You wanna work it out for a bit, lil' man?" Chang asked.

"Sure," Ajani answered.

"You don't talk much, do you? That's alright, lil' man. Still waters run deep. Take off your sneakers and get ready."

Chang started to shuffle his feet from side to side and front to back.

"Keep your eyes on my feet. They're gonna get real blurry. It's like three-card Monte, Ajani. Which foot is it gonna be? Which one's gonna get ya?"

I could see that the boy was mesmerized.

Chang kept shuffling his feet before blasting the black heavy bag with a sidekick. I watched the two work the bag as Chang began teaching Ajani his first kung fu position—horse stance.

Another generation, I thought.

22

"You suck at shootin', nigga." Ajani taunted Pedro. "I win again."

"Whatever. You think you hot shit 'cause you could hit a basket? Let's play one more time and see what happens. I'm gonna get physical now."

Pedro stripped the ball from Ajani's hands and looked over at Chris Parker, who was sitting on a bench eating a ham sandwich. "Yo, Chris! Watch me school this black motherfucker!" Pedro checked the ball to Ajani and said, "Losers first."

"We know who just lost. But I'll start it up," Ajani said.

The two battled on the concrete court in East River Park as Chris Parker sat on the side, watching. He laughed as Ajani mopped the floor with his shorter, pudgier opponent.

Sometimes Ajani toyed with Pedro by shooting outside two pointers and other times driving right into him, making sure to give a stealth elbow to the gut before dropping in an easy lay-up.

Even though it was the end of December, Pedro still managed to stain his red T-shirt with plenty of sweat.

Ajani hit one more shot off the check-ball, which ended the game.

"Whatever, yo," Pedro said. "One of these days, I'm gonna get ya. And when that happens, yo, I'm gonna make you kneel to the new king on these fuckin' courts." He picked up the ball and shoved it to Ajani.

"That ain't *never* happenin'," Chris Parker chimed in. "Never ever."

Ajani and Pedro grabbed their coats and quickly put them on. The three boys picked up their bikes, walked to the East River, veered left, and headed to the Mound at the end of the promenade. Soon they were squeezing through the hole in the fence that was hidden by the tall bushes.

"Dirty-ass pigeons!" said Pedro, noticing a few standing on the flat stones next to him. "Shoo! Get the fuck outta here, ya flyin' rats!"

The pigeons didn't budge.

"I swear," Pedro continued, "I'm gonna stomp one of these filthy things out. Teach 'em a lesson."

"Don't!" yelled Ajani. "Leave 'em alone. What are you? Stupid?"

"Whatever, Ajani. You don't own me, yo." Pedro backed away from the crew of birds and pulled out a brittle blunt that he had rolled up earlier. Handing it to Ajani, he said, "Light this shit up."

"Did you take out the seeds and stems this time?" Chris Parker asked.

"Yeah, nigga," Pedro said. "I told you that wasn't my fault last time, yo. That *whole bag* we got last time was stems and seeds. This one's all good."

Ajani cautiously took a few puffs on the thin, crudely-rolled blunt. "I can't decide if I like this shit or not," he said, passing it along.

Pedro took a big drag, trying to hold the hit in, but coughed it out instead. His eyes started to water as he tried to catch his breath. "I know," he said. "We smoked, like, ten times so far, and I don't think I've gotten high yet. What the fuck?"

"Please," said Chris Parker as he grabbed the blunt. "You high right now, idiot. Look at your eyes. They red as fuck."

"Whatever, yo. I'm tellin' ya I ain't never been high yet."

"Yeah, sure," Chris Parker said. "Anyway, Ajani, have you seen Felix yet?"

"Nah, but I will tomorrow." Ajani took the blunt.

"We been goin' through these eight-balls mad quick," Pedro bragged. "Maybe we should start gettin' more. These fiends is like Cookie Monsters for this shit."

"Yeah," Chris Parker said, "just make sure you ain't *doin'* any of that shit. You see what it does to these guys. Fuckin' fiends."

"Whatever, yo. I heard this shit makes the bitches take their clothes off," Pedro said. "You just put a line down in front of 'em, and it's on. And I heard that you fuck good on coke, too."

"You wouldn't know about that shit, though, would you?" Chris Parker said with a snicker. "Yo, Ajani. You heard what I just said?"

But he hadn't. Ajani was staring at the dark blue sky with the blunt dangling between his fingers. He watched as a plane from LaGuardia jetted upward from the northeast, high above the Queensboro Bridge.

"Yo, Ajani!" Chris Parker shouted.

"Huh?"

"What the fuck you always lookin' up in the sky for?" asked Pedro. "You lookin' for UFOs and shit?"

"Nah," Ajani answered quietly. "I just like watchin' the planes that are headin' outta the city."

"You ever been on one?" Chris Parker asked.

"Nope. Not yet," Ajani answered, flicking the end of the blunt into the murky river. "I wanna talk about what happened with Al the other day. What are we gonna do about that?"

"What you mean, what we gonna do about that shit?" Pedro asked, annoyed. "We gonna get another piece, nigga. *That's* what. And if we see that bitch-boy again, we'll pull that shit out on him again."

"You sound mad ignorant, Pedro."

"Why? What's *your* brilliant idea, huh?"

"I don't got a brilliant idea," Ajani said, looking over at the pigeons. "All I'm sayin' is, you can't be pullin' a gat out every time we have an issue with someone. And we gotta make sure people don't got problems with our product. I don't wanna be confronted all the time."

"Especially when it's these older dudes," Chris Parker added. "Those guys don't play around."

"I ain't afraid of *none* of these suckas," Pedro proclaimed. "I'm for real, yo."

"Okay, killer," Chris Parker mocked. "Just don't be cuttin' the blow that much from now on."

"I got ya, man. But enough about that shit, yo." Pedro waved them both off. "So how we gonna get another piece?"

"My cousin got popped," Chris Parker said. "He's in Rikers. My mama said he's gonna be there for a while. So that ain't gonna work again. Who else do we know?"

Pedro cleared his voice. "Ajani, what about askin' B?"

Ajani was looking up at the sky again. He noticed a jet to the right, with its landing lights shining brightly, headed for JFK. Then, looking over at Pedro, he shook his head. "Yo, man. Sometimes you're dumber than you look. And that's hard to believe, 'cause you look dumb as hell. You know Byron won't be down with that shit. He'd probably whoop my ass. He already warned me to stop messin' with y'all."

Pedro threw a stone at the pigeons, scattering them in the air.

"Why? What's wrong with *me*?" Pedro said. "I'm a *great*— Oh, no! Motherfucker! One of those nasty-ass birds just shat on me!"

"Calm down," Ajani said, trying not to laugh. "It could be good luck."

"Calm down?! Those dirty fucks carry AIDS!"

"No, they don't," Ajani said. "It's just shit."

"Yeah. And at least you're used to it, Shade-dro," said Chris Parker. "We be shittin' on you every day, nigga."

As Pedro wiped the droppings off his shoulder, he said, "For real, though. How we gettin' another gun, yo?"

Chris Parker looked at Ajani. "What about Primo?"

23

"What are you doing?" I asked Jack Woo.

He was in his cramped kitchenette with a heated wok on the stove.

"Don't worry, playa. I've done this many a time. The trick is to keep the burner on low. Don't get too impatient and turn the heat up all the way."

Woo held a small glass bottle of ketamine over the wok and poured the clear liquid out. I had never seen this technique performed before and was skeptical, but I knew that Jack was a K-scholar.

Primo was staring out the living room window, which overlooked Washington Square Park. The trees were bare, and most of the grass was gone, but the fake Rastas were still out slinging drugs to passing students.

"Can you hear the sizzle?" Jack asked.

The liquid had quickly solidified into what looked somewhat like a fried egg white.

"Holy shit!" I said in disbelief.

"Yep. You learn something new every day, right?" Jack grabbed the wok and slid the thin disc of K onto a clean plate. "Voila! There you have it!" He was quite proud of himself. "Now just get a blade and start chopping." He put the wok back on the stove to let it cool off.

"Damn!" said Primo in genuine amazement. "I've seen people bake this shit, steam it, or even sun-dry it. But *this*, I've never seen before."

The three of us sat down on the soft microsuede couches in the living room. Next to me, lying on his back with his legs kicked up in the air, was a large gray pit bull. His tongue was hanging out, and all of his teeth were showing as I rubbed his belly.

"Yo," Jack Woo said. "Zeus is standoffish with most people. He's way into you, though, B. Ya know, dogs can sense fucked-up energy. That's how I know you're a chill motherfucker."

"No doubt," I said, petting away. "He turns into a pile of mush around me, but I wouldn't wanna test him. I bet he's fierce as fuck."

"That's why I got the big boy. He looks bad walking down the ave in his spiked collar and *this*." Woo held up a super thick metal chain that he used as a leash.

"I bet," I said.

Primo said nothing. He was focused on dicing up the drugs into a fine powder with a sharp blade.

Woo busted out a straw and turned on his stereo. "Yo, Raekwon killed it with the second *Purple Tape*. This is the best sequel album *ever*." He proclaimed this as he cut the straw into two pieces and handed one to Primo. "Still on heavy rotation," he added.

"Hell, yeah," Primo said before taking a huge gagger. "Turn that shit up! The beats are just bananas!"

When it was my turn with the plate, I didn't dare take a rail like Primo's. I started smaller because I knew from experience that the K-hole is deep and dark.

It didn't take long, just a few minutes. The drip that ran down my throat was sharp. It was a sign that I was about to get bent. That sort of got me excited. It's a tricky high, though, varying from time to time. Euphoric and introspective on occasions. But queasy and robotic on others.

Things around me slowed to a crawl. My hearing was fine-tuned, but the music still seemed to go off-tempo at points, playing tricks on me. All I could do was try to pull the notes back together until they were in the right rhythm once again.

"Yeah, boy," Jack Woo said, satisfied, tilting his head all the way back and resting it against the top of his couch. "Now, *that's* pure. Most of these kids are getting that table salt from India, but I still like cooking it up the old-fashioned way."

As the music played on, we listened silently to hard off-kilter beats and minor chords.

"My life is fucked," Primo announced abruptly, with no particular emotion. He stared at the dog next to me. "Just like Zeus over there—eat, shit, sleep.

No one responded.

"At least the dog doesn't feel guilty about doin' nothin' productive," Primo added. "*He's* the lucky one."

"C'mon, Primo, it ain't that bad," I said. "Lighten up. You just gotta find somethin' you wanna do. A passion. Ya know?"

"Passion?" Primo said with a snicker. "What if your passion is illegal? Then what?"

"Maybe think of somethin' else, then," I answered, as if that were so simple.

"What else am I gonna be? I can't think of one thing." He snorted more K. "Yet, I know that I *don't* wanna be almost *everything*."

"What about me?" Jack said. "I graduated from NYU almost ten years ago. Cost my parents an arm and a leg. And I *still* don't know what I wanna do for a living. Now, *that's* no direction."

"Our generation was written off," Primo complained. "We're slaves, indentured servants to a failing corrupted sys... system..." His voice trailed off at the end. He was going out there.

"I think you might've had too much of that mumble sauce," Jack Woo said, pointing to the plate on the coffee table in front of us. "Maybe we should do some more." He grabbed the plate and started cutting a few lines.

"Where does this lead?" Primo asked.

"Huh?" I said.

"That journey Penny told us about? Where does mine go? Nowhere. Eat. Shit. Sleep."

Everybody respected Primo when we were growing up. Young birds would flock to him because he was good-looking. I admired the way he carried himself—his swagger. So I would take mental notes on how to play certain situations by watching what he would do. Primo back then was something to see, boy. And I had a front-row seat.

Like the night we were driving on the West Side Highway after a Jane's Addiction concert. Fifteen and fucked up—me, Primo, and a couple friends were in the hatchback. We lit up a joint and soon got pulled over.

"Holy shit, Bif!" I blurted from the back seat. "Bif, stop! Yo, put that out!"

The cop tapped assertively on the driver's side. Big Bif rolled down the window as commanded and exhaled smoke right into the officer's scowling round face. Trying not to, the cop coughed ever so slightly. The shit was too good.

"Did you see that red light right there, boy?" the officer asked Bif in a low bass.

"I did, but—"

"No!" the cop barked, as if the question were rhetorical. "You *didn't* see the red light, 'cause you was too busy smokin'."

"Officer, sorry about that," Primo said without wavering. "It's just that we went to see a show and decided to get a little treat, ya know? And after the show was over, we had some left. So, you see, sir, we just wanted to finish what we had before we got home."

"Yeah, *and?*" By now the cop was leaning in the window.

"Would you wanna finish the rest of this so we don't have to?"

My jaw dropped. Primo was so smooth, it was ridiculous. So confident with the plan he was working. He was Joe Cool.

The officer pushed back his helmet, revealing his receding curly black hair. Scratching his light brown freckled cheek, he looked Primo in the eye, and said, "Fine, hand it over."

Primo pulled out a fifty bag, which had the words *Hawaiian Skunk* printed on both sides, and handed it over to the cop.

"Now give me the jay."

Bif handed over what was left of the joint.

"I could've fucked with you big time tonight," the officer warned Bif. Looking at the rest of us, he said, "I could've fucked you *all* tonight. Yep, right in the ass! Consider this a get-out-of-jail-free card from the NYPD."

I will never forget what happened next. The cop looked over at Primo riding shotgun, gave a nod, and said, "Alright, guy. Thanks."

Thanks? Can you believe that? We get caught blowing a hit right in this cop's face, and by the time it's all over, he ends up *thanking* Primo! For me, it was something magical to watch.

When the light turned green again, the cop rode off into the night, and Primo pulled out another fifty. "Yo, B. You wanna roll this up? Fuck that freckled Morgan Freeman motherfucker."

That was Primo—good looks, calm, cool, and collected. I really looked up to him.

The Primo sitting next to me in Jack Woo's pad was unshaven, with bags under his eyes. He was popping Xanax and Percocets as if they were fucking Skittles. We used to pop all sorts of pills for fun when we were younger, but this was a different animal altogether. Who knows what else he was doing behind my back, too embarrassed to let me see?

Like an artery slowly becoming clogged, the damage forming day-to-day in Primo went unnoticed by me. The wear and tear crept up gradually. My best friend seemed fried, like the K in the wok. A foggy mind hovering above a disillusioned soul, feeling life's stress closing in on him. Stress that his potential has been slipping away like drops from a leaky faucet. Right down the fucking drain. Sadly, I'm not that different.

I was parched and needed a drink. In the kitchen, I pulled out a Brita pitcher from the fridge, filled three glasses with water, and handed one to each of my buddies back in the living room. Then I filled Zeus's bowl. He sprinted right over and started lapping up the water.

"I brought that herb, Woo," Primo said quietly, slowly opening his eyes. He walked over to his backpack by the front door, pulled out a sealed plastic bag, and handed it to Jack. "That's the shit I was tellin' you about the other day. Strawberry Cough."

"Whoo, baby! Excellent! Thirty-two for the half-pound, right?"

Primo nodded. "Don't tell anyone the deal I'm givin' ya," he said. "That's the family price, aight?"

"Of course, homie."

Jack reached into a white cardboard box on the floor and pulled out a shrink-wrapped six-pack of yellow ketamine boxes, each containing a single bottle. "And you wanted this, right?"

"Yeah, for sure," Primo said. "Just take it off what you owe me for the ganja."

Jack pulled out a wad of money from his pocket, licked his thumb, and began counting while Primo and I took turns doing more lines.

24

The following afternoon, I met up with Ajani. We walked over to Whole Foods on Houston, grabbed a green basket, and headed to the soup bar.

"Here," I said, ladling some butternut squash soup into a paper cup. "Try this. It's vegan. You know what that means? It means there's no animal parts in this soup. Just vegetables and good stuff like that. You got me?"

"Yeah." The boy peered into the oversized stainless steel pot full of steaming orange purée.

"You like butternut squash?" I asked. "You ever try squash?"

He shrugged his shoulders.

"Well, you're gonna try it now. That's exciting shit. That's one more vegetable to check off the list. This soup has vitamin A and iron. You see how bright and orange it looks? Perfect for the cold. Here, smell that." I put the steaming ladle under his nose. He took a whiff and nodded. "It's also got riboflavin. You know what *that* is?"

"No."

"Me, neither. It sounds cool, though, right? Riboflavin. Most importantly, the soup tastes good, my dude."

I popped a plastic lid on top of the container and put it in the basket. We continued to walk. Our next mission was to get some sandwich materials and juice.

"Yo, B," Ajani started. "How many girls have you slept with? I mean, not slept next to, but ya know—screwed?"

I smiled. My young pal had caught me off guard. I respected his candor, though.

"I don't screw girls anymore, Ajani. Now it's women. And screwin' is just for sometimes. Sometimes you make love. Why you askin'? You got a shorty you've been scopin' out?"

"No... I mean, sort of."

"What's her name?"

"Janet."

"Janet. So, have you talked to her yet?"

"No."

"So, what's the problem? You afraid?"

He was silent and didn't defend himself.

"Nooooo," I answered for him. "I know this bad boy over here, who packs toolies, ain't afraid of no females. You're too mean for that, lil' man."

Ajani quietly went about selecting a loaf of seven-grain bread from the baked goods aisle. He didn't like getting teased.

"Have you ever kissed a girl?" I asked. "And I don't mean a peck like you would give your auntie or something. I mean open mouth, on the lips."

"No."

"What about your friends at school? What do they say?"

"My friend Chris Parker said that he got a hand job once."

"What about the fat one?"

"Pedro?"

"Whatever."

"He said he got some from this girl he got wasted on vodka. He said they might say no at first, but to keep getting them shots till they say yes. I think he's full of shit, though."

"I agree."

We made our way to the produce section to get some lettuce and tomatoes.

"The key is just being yourself. *And* makin' sure your self isn't a fuckin' schmuck. Do you know what a schmuck is?"

"No."

"It means a prick. You don't wanna be like that. Be kind. And make sure you show this girl respect. You know that song, 'Respect'? R-E-S-P-E-C-T?"

"Yeah," Ajani answered quickly. "Aretha Franklin."

"That's right. Just remember, though, Otis Redding wrote that song. A man demanding respect from his woman. It goes both ways." I grabbed two tomatoes and held them in front of me. "Male and female—two halves of a single whole. And you know what happens when they join together?"

"What?"

"Ketchup, stupid. Now let's go get some."

As I put the tomatoes in a produce bag, I could tell Ajani was marinating on what I had told him.

"You always had that little bad streak in you, Ajani," I said. "You know that? I got that, too. That's one of the parts of me that I see in you. I noticed that when I used to babysit you. Back then you only reached up to here." I held my hand down by my waist. "Your mom would go to work the nightshift, and you would just raise hell. I remember this one time I came back from the kitchen, and you had just jumped barefoot right through your mom's plate glass side table. I almost had a heart attack. You were standing there unscathed in a floor full of smoked glass shards with a fuckin' smirk on your face. Like you were sayin', *I ain't scared. Let's see you try it.* I could tell in that moment that we were two peas from the same pod. Buddies for life."

Ajani smiled.

"What I'm tryin' to say, lil' man, is that girls like a bad streak, but don't be a lowlife. Just keep outta trouble and keep goin' to school. You'll get the type of girl that will make you happy. It's up to you in the end." I grabbed his arm. "Remember, though, and this is the most important thing I can say—you don't fuck raw, okay? You wear a condom. Always. You don't need a fuckin' baby at your age, ya know? Or some virus that will burn your thing off."

The boy nodded that he understood.

"But one step at a time, alright?" I added.

"Did *you* always wear a condom?" he asked.

"No." My mind raced through flings from the past. "But I'm not necessarily proud of that. And this isn't about me. I did what I did already. This is about *your* turn around the block."

"Did you always love the girl you did it with?"

I laughed. "No."

"But you love Cecilia, right?"

I blushed. "I suppose I do. But that's not always enough to make it work. Listen, don't you worry about that. You're young. Have fun. A lot of it. But be intelligent, be cool, and the birds will flock to you. You got me?"

"Yeah." Ajani paused in thought. "I like her—Cecilia. Just wanted to let you know that I approve. Try to make it work."

"Thanks. I'll try. You're a lil' pimp, my man. Watch. You're gonna talk to this girl... um ... what's her name again?"

"Janet!"

"Right. Janet. You might actually have to tongue-kiss her, though. You ready for that, lil' bad boy? Sweet lil' street thug?"

We headed to the cash registers.

25

"So, how have you been, Byron?"

Penny's hair was in a bun. Her crimson merino sweater was frayed and dulled from too many turns in the washing machine. She's probably been wearing it since the early '80s. Hell, maybe even earlier.

"Ya know how it is, Penny," I said. "I'm just tryin' to get by in this foul world."

"Stop it, Byron," she said, slapping my hand. "You're starting to sound too much like Primo. You're blessed and you know it."

"Yeah, B," Cecilia said. "*I'm* here with you, right? Of course you're blessed."

"I like her already," Penny said with a grin. "You are blessed in so many ways. But you don't look at it that way—now, do you?"

A waitress with spiked, polka-dotted hair came over to take our order. We were sitting in Kate's Joint, the only vegetarian diner in Alphabet City, and unfortunately, it was closing for good any day now. Punk rock music was blasting, and all the waitresses looked like they had been rolled over by the band. It was almost eight hours since I had eaten soup and sandwiches with Ajani, so I was starving.

"What can I get for you tonight?" the waitress asked, sounding as if she couldn't care less.

We took turns ordering, making sure we got plenty to eat.

"Not really," I said when the waitress was gone.

"Not really *what*?" asked Cecilia.

I took a sip of Sprite. "Penny asked me if I look at my life as a blessing. And I say no. Not most of the time. More often I think to myself, what's the point? Conflict. Struggle. What's the fuckin' point of it all?"

"How can you say that, B?" asked Cecilia. "Look at all the things you have. You have people that care about you. You have your health. You have youth. You have intelligence. And you have a conscience."

"That's not enough."

"What do you mean *that's not enough*?" Cecilia asked impatiently.

"I mean, I want more than that," I answered calmly.

"And you feel you've somehow been cheated in the game of life? Is that it?" Penny said. "Let's all shed a tear for poor ol' Byron. He's not getting what he wants from this life. But, ah, do you even *know* what you want? Maybe what you want is right in front of you, and you can't even recognize it."

"Maybe," I said, taking another sip of soda.

The waitress came back with our steaming appetizers and placed them on the table. "Anything else?"

"No, we're good. Thanks," I answered.

Penny was staring at me intently.

"Listen," I said, "all I can say is that when my brother died, something sparked inside me. I feel like I have to change now, or I never will. And if I don't change, I'll regret it forever. But I don't know what changes to make. It's all too hazy."

"Yeah, I bet," said Penny.

"So, what do you want, Byron?" asked Cecilia. "Why don't you tell us?"

"I guess I don't know."

"Yes, you do," Penny said. "It's just that you can't see it clearly. Be honest with yourself. Truly honest. Like I said before, it's right in front of you."

I lifted up my plate and looked underneath it. Then I slid my

Sprite out of the way.

"What's in front of me?" I asked, acting confused.

"I'm serious, B. Stop being a wiseass." Penny gave me a hard look.

"You think I wanna be a writer? Like that's the missing puzzle piece of my life?"

"Perhaps," Penny said. "And perhaps not. Perhaps it's a wonderful steppingstone to help you get to the missing puzzle piece. That's for you to figure out. Just make sure you *do* figure it out. And you know how you do that?"

"How?"

"You figure it out by trying. Boom! There it is. Ain't so mystical of an answer, is it?"

Cecilia covered her mouth, chuckling quietly.

"You're not meant to just hustle on this island," Penny said. "That much I know, Byron."

A busboy cleared away the appetizers just as the waitress was bringing our entrées. "Here you go," she said flatly. "The plates are hot."

"Hmm," I said sarcastically when she was gone. "She really enjoys her job."

"Smartass," Cecilia said.

"Don't you wanna enjoy *your* job, Byron?" Penny asked. "Isn't that what we're talking about here? Some sort of career? Don't you wanna wake up most days feeling like you have some purpose?"

"Penny, what do you want me to say? You think I have some future in writing? I can't do it. I'm too—"

"You're too scared," Cecilia interrupted. "I don't know where that comes from, but I don't like it one bit. You have to follow through with your dreams, especially if you have talent. You just need the drive, and there'll be no stopping you."

"I *really* like this one, B. She's a keeper," Penny said. "Or how do you kids say it on the streets these days? Wifey material?"

She got that right.

"Just understand," Penny said, "you can't be so set in your ways.

Take a chance. Be firm but flexible."

"Like the willow," I mumbled.

"What?" Penny asked.

"Like the willow. Firm yet flexible. That's how the willow survives harsh winds."

"Let's toast to the willow!" Penny said.

We raised our glasses in unison and clanked them.

A little later, seeing our empty plates, the waitress asked, "Will that be it for tonight?"

"Yes," I said. "Just the check."

She put our check down and headed to the next table.

"Look, B," Penny said, "I'm not saying to stop what you're doing. I know you need to pay the rent." She gave me a wink. "Just work on your craft as often as you can, okay? I want you to send me a few of your stories. But this time with a beginning, middle, and end. Hopefully I can send you back some notes on how to improve them. I'll help you, but *you* have to take the initiative to help yourself. Got me?"

I looked at Cecilia. She was gorgeous, but her stone-cold stare told me, *Say yes already!*

So I said, "I got you, Penny. You win, alright?"

"You still don't fully get it, do you, *bubbeleh*?" Penny said, pushing up her glasses. "You're taking your destiny in your own hands, B. That makes *you* the winner."

26

Primo leaned back on the dusty corduroy couch. It was so cluttered that he had to clear off some old magazines just to make room for himself. He was in a living room surrounded by outdated '70s wallpaper and tan shag wall-to-wall carpeting. The shades were pulled, and the room was dimly lit.

A man with an olive complexion walked out of the bedroom, dressed only in a wifebeater, boxers, and a beige silk robe. His potbelly pushed out, making his chest look sunken in comparison. He had a thin mustache, but body hair as thick as wool.

"Hey, Primo! *Qué pasa, mi pana?*"

"Just gettin' by, Javier, ya know."

Primo's stomach was rumbling from the Oxycontin he had crushed up and snorted after scraping off the time-release coating. His neck was starting to itch.

Javier grabbed a spoon-shaped glass pipe from on top of the TV. The outside of the pipe was colored with different shades of blue, but the inside was completely filled with white resin. He lit up, took a few puffs, exhaled, and then put the pipe down.

Reaching over to the table next to the TV, he grasped a black .44 Magnum with scope included, opened the cylinder, and looked inside to make sure the chambers were loaded. There was a loud click as he smacked the barrel back in place. With a cockeyed look, he pointed the gun at Primo and peered through the scope.

"What the fuck's wrong with you? I don't like those shits being pointed at me, aight?"

Javier twisted the large revolver sideways, continuing to aim it at Primo's head with one eye closed. Then he dropped his arm. "What the fuck is up *your* asshole, shit-for-brains? Don't come in here talkin' that way. In here, *I'm* king. And *this*," he spread his arms wide, "this is my castle! *El* fuckin' *rey*. Got me?"

"Yeah, I got ya."

"I'm not so sure, Primo. Sometimes you could be a real simpleton." Javier's glassy eyes looked directly into Primo's. "Yeah, I'm not so sure ya got me. Here, I'm gonna show ya what I'm talkin' about... Lisa!" He shouted at the top of his lungs. "Lisa! Get your ass out here, baby! *Ven aca, mami!*"

Primo could hear the click-clacking of high heels approaching.

"Yes, *papi*. What can I do for you?" asked Lisa. Her hair was big, and so were her hips.

"Go to the store and get me some Ritz crackers and a lemon icy. Ya got me, bitch?"

"Yes, *papi*."

"Ya want anythin', Primo?"

"No, I'm fine. Thanks."

"Time ain't stopped right now, baby. Chop-chop!" Javier barked, clapping his hands. "*Avanza*, bitch! I'm hungry!"

Lisa scuffled away in her heels right out the door.

"Ya see how I roll, Primo? How I do?"

"I got ya, Javier. Damn, man. You didn't have to get your bitch to go out and—"

"Whoa, whoa, whoa, *maricón*. Don't be callin' my sexy Latina queen no bitch. *Entiendes*?"

"What the fuck? You just called her a bitch and ran her outta here for some crackers and an icy," Primo said, defending himself. "Fuck it, I'm sorry. She ain't a bitch, aight?"

"So, what ya want anyway?"

"I want another two bottles of Oxys and another half of that

Colombian. What the hell do ya *think* I want?"

"Easy. Calm down. Damn, you really have some anger issues to work out," Javier said as he grabbed the pipe for another puff. "And, ya know, *amigo*, you should really slow down on all those pills and shit. They'll kill ya."

Primo shook his head in disbelief. "Do you have more or not, Javier? I got a thing," he said, tapping the invisible watch on his wrist.

Javier tied his robe over his protruding belly and headed into the kitchen, where he opened a cabinet and pulled out a couple of script bottles with the information scratched off. From another cabinet, he pulled out a bag of white powder. Then he returned to the living room, and threw the two plastic bottles and the bag of coke down on Primo's lap.

"I had everything prepared for ya already. Call it addict intuition. *Intuición.*"

Primo stuffed the drugs into his jacket pockets and looked up at Javier, who was staring at him.

"What's up?" Primo asked.

"You know what the fuck's up, you slick bastard. *El dinero, pendejo!* Where is it? You already owe me, like, seven grand for *las píldoras* and the yayo. Now you take more. How are ya plannin' to make this right? I'm gonna start chargin' interest on your ass!"

"Just let me figure it out, Javi, and get back to ya the next time I see ya."

"No, no, no, Primo. I don't think so. You keep doin' that same song and dance. No more. You're gonna figure it out right now before you leave here. *Tu me entiendes?*"

Primo glanced at the loaded Magnum on the counter. "I know how to get the money," he said after a brief silence. "I know someone who has some valuable shit I might be able to acquire. Fuck, I can stand to make a buck, too."

"Now you're thinkin' with your brain." Javier took another hit from his crack pipe. "I know a couple *cabrones* who can probably help ya with your situation. That's if you *need* help."

"Oh, yeah?"

"Yeah. The Balducci brothers. Sal and Slim. They're pretty good with helpin' people out of a jam."

"Yeah, I could probably use some help."

"I'll put ya in touch with Sal. He'll give ya a call. Trust me."

"No doubt. I'll make somethin' happen."

"Just make sure you take care of that by the next time I see you, *pendejo*. Ya don't want me to send the hyenas after your ass. Hyenas chomp through bone."

Primo stood up and walked toward the front door.

"So just do both of us a favor and don't fuck up," Javier said, pointing his Magnum at the back of Primo's head.

27

"Hey, Zev!" I called out. "Happy New Year!"

He was on the corner of Kent Avenue and North 10th Street in Williamsburg, wearing the same outfit he always wore—a black suit and shiny black shoes with a white button-down and matching shawl.

"*Shalom*, B," said the Jew. "Actually, *we* go by a different calendar. Come. It's frigid."

"This chill won't let up," I added, shaking my head.

The round penguin-man waddled in front of me and unlocked the door to a massive stone loft building.

The space we entered inside was raw and completely unfinished. Scraps of sandpaper, tools, and wooden planks were lined up against one of the walls. The daylight brightened up the loft naturally, but the heat was off and the open space was very cold.

"What's up with *this* spot?" I asked.

"I own this building, B. It's a work in progress, as you can tell."

"This is a lotta space," I said as I looked around. "What's gonna go in here?"

Zev shrugged. "Not sure yet. Why? You interested?"

"Maybe one day. Need to build up some more capital first."

"So let me help you. What do you have?" He straightened his yarmulke, which had slid to the left.

I took off my backpack, unzipped it, and pulled out a plump vacuum-sealed bag. "Sour Diesel," I said proudly.

"Yes! Let's try some!" He took off his thick glasses and rubbed them clean on the end of his shawl.

The whole room immediately started to stink, the minute I ripped the bag open.

"It smells like lemon zest. *Otzer n'shiymah*," the Jew said, wafting the air toward his nose.

"What does that mean?" I asked.

"Breathtaking!"

Pulling out a king-size rice paper, I quickly rolled up a massive joint, lit the tip, and started to smoke. After a moment, I passed the jay over to Zev while trying not to cough.

The Jew took a hit and blew steam out of his nostrils.

"What do ya think?" I asked.

"I think I'm already high. *Real* high." He grabbed the pound of Sour and waved it in front of me. "My friends are going to just be blown away. *That's* what I think. Thank you so much, B." He walked over to an unfinished closet, put the herb away, and pulled out a few stacks of cash. "Eight thousand, right?"

"Yup." I took a hit from the king-sized joint.

He handed me one stack with five thousand and another with three.

"I'll make sure Golden gets some of that for hookin' us up," I said as I put away the money.

"Good. I know he'll come looking if you don't."

"Can I ask you something?" The weed had me open.

"Of course, B."

"Do you believe in the Torah? I mean, do you believe in Adam and Eve?" I felt silly asking Zev that question, but I continued. "It seems a little ridiculous to me."

"I believe in faith," Zev answered quickly. Taking the joint from me, he added, "Faith in things that seem correct in my heart. As for the First Testament and the stories it contains—I guess the short answer is no. No, I don't think the story of Adam and Eve is to be taken literally. But, B, in every ancient tale there are grains of truth and lessons to be learned. Nevertheless, I absolutely believe that there is one true god, and that Jews are the chosen people."

"But how can you just believe blindly in something that hasn't clearly revealed itself to you?"

"We do it all the time, B. Heck, our lives are *built* on blind faith. If blind faith is having full trust in something that is unknown, then isn't it blind faith to merely assume that we are going to rise to see another morning? To plan one's life as if we are going to make it to the finish line? Seems like blind faith to me."

"That's not the same thing, though," I argued.

"Let me try another path. When you have a tough decision to make, yes or no, what do you do?"

"I guess I try to weigh both options and pick the one my gut tells me to."

"Well, wouldn't you say that you have faith in your decision being the correct one? You don't *know* whether it is or isn't. In fact, once you choose one direction and see an outcome, you'll never know what the other outcome would have been. You have faith in your choices that deal with the unknown future ahead of you, and you have faith that there will even *be* a future."

"I still don't think that's the same thing as believing in god and superstitions. I think science is more accurate and truthful than religion has ever been."

"That may be true, but let me ask you this, B." He again wiped his glasses clean on the tip of his white shawl and placed them back on his face. "Why?"

"Why *what*?"

"Why? No matter what scientific conclusions, you can always ask why. Inevitably, there comes a point when science can no longer answer the why. There is no answer at that point, B. Or at least no answer we can comprehend. After all, any scientists worth their weight would tell you that they know only a small part of what is really going on out there. We children of the almighty actually know very little about ourselves and our surroundings."

"I know my surroundings just fine." I passed him what was left of the joint.

"Really?" Zev puffed on the roach one last time before putting it out with his loafer. "I'm not sure you know *these* surroundings."

"What do you mean?"

"Follow me."

I followed Zev to the opposite end of the loft.

"You ready?" he asked, grabbing a door handle in front of him.

"Ready for what?"

"For *this*."

As he opened the door, I was instantly blinded.

"Not bad, huh, B?" he said, leading the way into the bright room.

"Is this all yours?"

"Of course. To whom else would it belong?"

A dozen-plus lights hung from chains in the ceiling, shining over long rows of plants, all uniform in size. A sea of green.

"I've never seen so many stalks," I said in a trance.

"There's about a hundred of them," Zev said proudly. "My first harvest. Any interest?"

"Well, god bless you, fine sir. In this life and the next."

28

Dolores ran a steamy shower, then sat on the toilet with the lid down. She took the last swig off a pint bottle of Beam and lit up a cigarette.

"Mama?" called Ajani from the other side of the bathroom door. "What do you want for dinner?"

Dolores took one more drag, flushed the cigarette down the toilet, and responded, "Anything you want, dear. How about Shanghai Gardens? You like their General Tso's, right?"

"Sure. What do *you* want?" He already had the phone in his hand, ready to order, and knew the number by heart. "Beef and broccoli again?"

"Sure, sweetie. Order me that."

She turned off the shower, put the empty bottle in the medicine cabinet behind the mirror, and frantically waved her hand in the air to clear the smoke. But her fanning just caused it to collect near the ceiling.

Ajani ordered the food and sat down in front of the TV in the living room. He was frowning, deep in thought, when his mother walked in and took a seat next to him. His nostrils flared as he smelled smoke on her.

"Oooh," she said. "Knicks, Nets? How's Melo playing tonight, huh?"

"Why are you doin' that stuff?" he asked frankly. "You know you don't have to."

Shocked, she grabbed the remote and turned off the TV. "Doing what?"

"Drinking so much. Is it 'cause of me?" He was looking straight ahead, rather than making uncomfortable eye contact with his mother.

As she tried desperately to stay focused, her throat clogged up. "No," she answered gently, "of course not, baby. I just... I just need some help getting through the day sometimes, sweetie. It helps me, ya know? Like medicine."

"Medicine?" Ajani sneered. His sadness was slowly giving way to anger.

Dolores was embarrassed and silent for a few seconds. Nausea spread rapidly through her midsection and made her wonder if she would vomit.

"Baby," she said, her bottom lip quivering, "your mama has some problems. I'm so sorry. But I just need help to get through the day." A tear ran down the woman's face from deep shame. She grabbed a tissue and asked, "Did I ever tell you about Poppy and Gammy?"

"Not much. What do *they* have to do with anything?"

"Baby, you're at a crucial point in your life. Hopefully you're at an age now where you can truly appreciate who they were. Where you come from. You might think that I'm a mess, but I want you to know that you come from something better than this. Better than me. I couldn't really talk to you about this before because you were just too young. But now I can see that you're becoming a man right in front of my eyes." She tenderly rubbed the top of her hand against Ajani's smooth cheek. "A handsome, thoughtful young black man. But I know you like to hang with your hoodlum friends on the block, too. You like getting into trouble. So did your father. In and out of prison for stupid, petty things. What did it ever get him? Get us? What did it ever get anyone? So... Poppy and Gammy."

The boy sat with anticipation, ready to hear more. He had never met his grandparents, since they had both died before he was born.

"Poppy's name was Carl," his mother continued, "and Gammy's name was Lorraine. They were part of a group called the Black Panthers. Have you ever heard of them?"

He shook his head.

"Schools still don't teach about Huey, huh? Let's just say they fought for black people's rights. You understand? Blacks didn't have real rights when your grandparents were your age. You think it's bad now? It was worse. Way worse. We were horribly mistreated. So your grandparents fought for equality. For their beliefs. They didn't concern themselves with ignorant bullshit. They were good, passionate people that cared. They made a difference in the world. That was your Poppy and Gammy."

"What about you?" Ajani asked.

"Well," Dolores hesitated, thrown off by the question. "A long time ago, before the grocery mart, I worked at a place called Safe Horizon. We helped battered women and children stuck in broken homes. It was so fulfilling, it really was." She wiped away another tear. "But when your father left me, I couldn't—" She started to cry, but then pulled herself together. "I had to take care of you all by myself. It was so scary. So lonely, Ajani. Anyway, one day, I got caught drunk on the job, and they told me not to come back."

"Did you ever try to stop?" Ajani asked.

Looking totally defeated, she reached for a new tissue and said, "Of course, sweetie. Many times. But I don't know, I always go back." She gazed at her son warmly. "Don't be embarrassed about your mama, okay? You're stronger than me. Always have been. Do you know what your name means, Ajani?"

The boy shook his head. "I didn't know it meant anything."

"It's an African name. It means—*he who wins the struggle.*"

Each word hit the impressionable young boy with authority.

Dolores continued, "See I knew you wouldn't just survive the game, Ajani, you were gonna win it. I knew it when I held you in my arms as a baby. I know it now." She caressed her son's leg. "And I want you to remember that, when you're up to no good," she added sternly. "Remember that you are to *win* the struggle, not lose it and end up getting put away for some nonsense. The last place a black man should *ever* be is behind bars. Got me, baby?"

Ajani let the new information soak into his skin like warm rays from a tropical sun. A new sense of pride took over his being. He saw his mother in a different light, a brilliant luminescence he had never seen before. She was good in the heart, and that was all that mattered.

"You have a lot to think about, young man," she said, kissing her son on the forehead. "Go to the bedroom and finish your homework until the Chinese food gets here. You can watch the rest of the game while you eat."

29

TAKE ME, I AM THE DRUG; TAKE ME, I AM
HALLUCINOGENIC.

—SALVADOR DALI

I TOOK THE ACID ABOUT TWO HOURS AGO.
AT FIRST THERE WAS AN UNEASY ANTICIPATION.
BUTTERFLIES IN MY STOMACH MADE IT DIFFICULT
FOR ME TO EAT OR DRINK ANYTHING EXCEPT
WATER. I JUST LISTENED TO PETER TOSH'S
WANTED DREAD AND ALIVE, WAITING FOR THE
HALLUCINOGEN TO KICK IN.

THE FIRST THING I NOTICED WAS MOVEMENT.
SLIGHT MOVEMENT IN INANIMATE OBJECTS. DULL
COLORS APPEARED MORE VIBRANT, ALMOST
GLOWING, AND SHAPES AND PATTERNS FELT
SACRED.

FOR BETTER OR FOR WORSE, I LIKE IT. NEW
INSIGHTS ENTER MY MIND AT WILL. RANDOM
REALIZATIONS. HINTS OF ENLIGHTENMENT. LIGHT
PULLING ME AWAY FROM THE SHADOWS. EVEN
THOUGH INTIMIDATING OR AWKWARD AT TIMES, IT'S
GOODNESS. AND WHEN IT IS ALL OVER, I FEEL
CLEANSED AND BRAND-NEW. MY PURE ESSENCE
BECOMES HUMBLE AND KIND.

TONIGHT, AS I TRY TO WRITE THESE WORDS ON

THIS SWIRLING PAPER, I THINK OF MY LIFE. WHAT THE HELL AM I DOING?

THESE TIMES OF UNCERTAINTY MAKE ME WANT TO SCREAM OUT TO THE WORLD, "I'M SCARED! YOU HEAR ME OUT THERE? I AM OVER-FUCKING-WHELMINGLY TERRIFIED OF THE FUTURE!" IT'S NO JOKE OUT THERE. IN THIS CRUEL UNFORGIVING CITY. HOW LONG CAN YOU BE A DREAM-CHASER BEFORE YOUR ASS IS OUT ON THE STREET?

DON'T GET ME WRONG—I DON'T SEE ANYTHING IMMORAL OR SINFUL ABOUT WHAT I DO. ABOUT SELLING WEED. SHIT, JUST ASK THE GREAT PEOPLE OF COLORADO. IT'S JUST THAT I DON'T FEEL RIGHT ANYMORE. I CRAVE MORE THAN THIS.

BUT WHY? WHO REALLY CARES ANYWAY? I AM LESS THAN A SPOT ON THE FABRIC OF TIME AND SPACE. LESS THAN A SPECK IN AN INCOMPREHENSIBLY VAST UNIVERSE. WE'RE ALL SO SMALL. SO INSIGNIFICANT. YET, SOMEHOW I GUESS I STILL FEEL SOME SORT OF SELF-WORTH. HUMANS CAN HAVE SUCH A MASSIVE EFFECT IN JUST ONE LIFETIME. WE ALL HOLD THE POWER TO INFLUENCE THE WORLD. THAT IS OUR SIGNIFICANCE. SIGNIFICANT. INSIGNIFICANT. THAT IS THE BALANCE. THE YIN AND THE YANG.

AM I BABBLING? I SHOULD STOP NOW ANYWAY, AS I CAN HARDLY KEEP WRITING. HARDLY SEE. THAT CAN ONLY MEAN ONE THING—IT'S TIME TO HIT UP THE CLUB AND GET SMASHED.

"Jah Rastafari!" shouted the DJ, who sported thick black dreadlocks and a goatee. He was standing in the corner on a platform with two turntables and a mixer in front of him. Sometimes he would grab a microphone to work the crowd.

"King Selassie ah di ruler! Him bust di seventh seal, and him build di school, and him educate di youths! Selassie I!"

My mind wandered. The room was smoky. Not from cigarettes, though, just sweet-smelling sensimilla. Occasionally a whiff of burnt seeds floated by, to my dismay.

The vinyl records crackled as they spun. Warm bass lines seemed to come out in rings that widened exponentially, creating large and ever-expanding sonic cones colored in electric blue. Choppy organ riffs filled the air, coming alive as visions of brilliant orange lasers, and zigzagged across the room in syncopation with the beat. With each chord played, another orange laser chased the one before it, first up and then down.

Primo and I were sitting with two Rastafarians in a tight area that was roped off. The room seemed to separate into sections that bobbed up and down as if we were floating on the ocean. I may have eaten too much L. All I could do was surrender to the flow.

We downed shots of Appleton rum and chased them with Red Stripes. To my left, Primo lit another oversized Marley cone. He was talking into the ear of one of the Rastas, whose dreads ran down the length of his entire back. The man's hair flopped around in all directions, covering much of his face. The dreads looked alive, like the snakes on Medusa's head, but I wasn't frightened. His skin was very dark. The weak lighting made him and his friend, who was silently nodding his head to the music, look even darker.

I was one of the only white boys in the crowd, but I didn't feel out of place. Quite the contrary. The dress code was casual, to say the least, and the mood was unpretentious. The music was *rebel* music.

Four Red Stripes and a few shots in my system, and I wasn't planning on quitting soon. I was lifted, my eyes bloodshot. As the DJ with the goatee blended one warm vibe into another, I caught myself drifting. Time slowed down. Some things seemed blurry, while others I could see with precision. Like a camera lens. In and out of focus. In and out. A woman at the bar caught my lens. I zoomed in. She had her thin dreads wrapped up vertically and covered with a silk scarf. After casually taking a shot of brown liquor, she twisted her body to the music. Sexy. I thought of Cecilia.

"Yo, B!" Primo yelled over the music. He was waving a joint in front of me. The glowing cherry at the tip of the spliff was spitting out tiny sparks that jumped at me before fizzling. "Earth to B! Here. Take this, homie. Super Silver. One of your favorites."

I took the joint and smoked until I coughed violently.

> *Don't kill him.*
> *Don't kill di lion.*
> *Don't kill him.*
> *Hear what I say?*
> *Don't kill him.*
> *Don't kill di lion.*
> *Don't kill him.*

Burning Spear was earnestly pleading in my ear. His unmistakable voice rang out of the speakers, taking the form of white light that continuously generated sacred geometry onto the back of my eyelids.

Primo stood up and headed to the bathroom. The dread he was talking to came and sat next to me. His smile was missing many teeth, which went along perfectly with his patchy beard and slight lazy eye. He cleared the serpent-like hair from his face and secured it with a hair tie that he was wearing above his red, gold, and green wristband. I was finally confident that a snake would *not* be biting me.

The man leaned into my ear and said, "Greetings, B. How've you been, bredren?" His voice was deep, his accent thick.

"How are ya, De'ron?" I asked as I sipped a beer bottle. "It's been a while since we last saw each other."

"I and I is glad you two came," he said.

"Thanks for the invite. I haven't been to the BX in a minute."

"Mi bredren, ah him own dis place. Him take care ah we. Some free drink and ting."

I've known De'ron for years. We used to smoke up by the music studio in Vinegar Hill. He'd play me old dubplates or brand new *riddims* he was working on. Honest and respectable, he's a solid guy, but not to be crossed. One day he shanked a man for disrespecting his wife and had to dip out of town for a while until things cooled off. It was good to see him again.

"How's it been?" I asked. "Heard you started a family since we last saw each other."

"Yes, I. Di likkle one. Him grow up fast, nuh *bloodclaatt*. It's a sight to behold. Seen?"

"I'm sure," I agreed.

Someone passed me the spliff. When I exhaled, the smoke mushroomed into an enormous balloon that floated away.

"How yuh likkle bredda?" asked the Ras. "Mi nuh see him since you carry him over by Puff Tuff. Over deh so by di river."

"My brother died this past summer." I took a swig of beer for Will. His face appeared so clearly in front of me.

De'ron hung his head in disbelief. "So sorry, B. Him way too young fi lef we suh." He paused. "But him still wit we. You see mi? Dat mi know."

"Thanks, my dude. I appreciate that. I'm just tryin' not to let the anger fuck my head up. I'm tryin' to stay strong, ya know?"

"You *are* strong, my youth," said De'ron. "You bun di sacrament. You eat *Ital* food. Most important, you come from di heart, bredren. Seen?" De'ron's face stretched out and shrank back down as if pulsating to his heartbeat. His broken smile turned serious as he continued, "And true you ah mi bredren, mi haffi tell you a ting. And mi ah tell you, B, mi nuh like it nah *bumbaclot*. So mi ah try fi nip it in di bud right now, family."

"What?" I asked. I could feel the stress start to stir in the pit of my stomach.

"Check it. Mi have dis dream a couple nights ago. Seen? And mi is a man weh my dreams are sent from di most high and tell mi tings."

"And?" I asked, confused.

"You was in dis dream, B. Betrayed like the Good Shepherd was betrayed by Judas Iscariot."

"By who?" I said, sitting up.

"Mi never know who. You haffi well sharp right now. Take no signs for granted. Look around, and make sure who you ah let in is worthy, bredda. Don't get a big *bumbaclot* head and misjudge people and dem intention. Seen? Some people will hate what you have, especially if dem nuh have no ting. Sin of mankind."

I nodded.

"And when you figure out who ah try fi dis yuh program, you done know seh dem *batty* bwoy fi get bullet! Mi respect what the I stand for, Byron." He softly jabbed his finger in my chest, his head still pulsating. "Not like di pussy-hole gangsta bwoys. Dem inna di streets wit nuh *bloodclaat* moral. Mi know seh, you have di overstanding, my youth." De'ron smiled, and just as quickly wiped it off his face. "Just keep dem eyes open fi di omen, and *Jah-Jah* will guide you. Mi ah tell you."

His voice consoled me. Plus, his friend was rolling another spliff of Silver Haze. It couldn't have come soon enough.

30

PEOPLE SAY BELIEVE HALF OF WHAT YOU SEE,
SON, AND NONE OF WHAT YOU HEAR.
I CAN'T HELP BEIN' CONFUSED.
IF IT'S TRUE PLEASE TELL ME DEAR.

  —MARVIN GAYE
   "I HEARD IT THROUGH THE GRAPEVINE"

NOW I SEE MOST CLEARLY. OR DO I STILL
CLEARLY SEE NOTHING? EVERYTHING IS AN
ILLUSION. SMOKE AND MIRRORS. MAKES A PERSON
WONDER WHAT THE FUCK THE POINT IS. WHY GO
ON? WHY FIGHT ANOTHER DAY? WHY NOT JUST
QUIT AND HIDE UNDER A ROCK SOMEWHERE? OR
SHOOT SOME DOPE AND TRY TO FIND NIRVANA?
  SOMEONE IS GONNA TRY TO ROB ME. PULL MY
CARD. MY SPIDEY SENSES ARE IN TUNE. LET HE
WHO WANTS WHAT I HAVE REVEAL HIMSELF. I CAN
SMELL A LIE. FEEL A FAKE. NOTHING WORSE THAN
A FAKE-ASS MOTHERFUCKER! HATE THEM ALL!
THAT'S WHY I LOVE PRIMO. NO MATTER WHAT SHIT
HE'S GETTING INTO, AT LEAST HE UNDERSTANDS
THE VALUE OF TRUTH.

The subway car shrieked obnoxiously as we rode home from the Rasta party by Yankee Stadium.

I put my journal in my back pocket.

It was just after seven in the morning, and my eyes were burning from no sleep. Primo was much luckier—passed out in front of me. A cutie with a cocoa complexion was snoring on his shoulder. Above them was a discolored sticker that read:

I CAN'T
AFFORD
TO ♥
NY

No fuckin' doubt, I thought to myself.

Jamaican rum and too many Silver Haze joints made me fade in and out, but traces of acid still had my head buzzing with thoughts and visions.

"Coming up, Broadway-Lafayette," a muffled voice said from the speakers overhead. "This is a Brooklyn-bound D train. Again, this is Broadway-Lafayette."

"Yo, Primo," I said, shaking his arm. "Yo, Primo, this is our stop. Let's go."

He opened his eyes with a confused look. "It's all good." His voice was dry. "I'm goin' to Natasha's. Take it easy, aight, homie?"

"That's cool," I said. "Be good, my dude."

I got out of the train and walked across the barren platform to wait for the F. Up a little ways from me, I saw a few bums sleeping upright on the hard benches. I knew there were plenty more homeless people asleep even deeper in the tunnels. Mole people.

"Excuse me, sir," a raspy voice said behind me.

I nervously turned around, my hands clenched into fists.

"Sorry to bother you, sir. But do you have sixty-seven cents?"

The man asking for change was no more than five feet tall, wearing a stained T-shirt that barely fit over his bloated gut. The smell of shit and cheap vodka emanated from his body. I felt bad, not only for him but for humanity.

"Sorry, pal."

"Please, sir. I need to get a drink. I only need sixty-seven more cents." The bum reached out his hand. He was wearing cloth gloves with the fingertips cut off, revealing his dirty, gnarled-up fingernails.

"Hold on," I said, pulling out my money clip and handing the smelly guy a fifty.

"Oh, bless you, my child!" the squat man said with wide eyes. His voice reverberated off the tiled walls. "Bless you."

"Sure," I said. "Just do me a favor. Clean yourself up somewhere, alright?"

"Will do." He started to make his way back to the benches.

I turned around to peer into the tunnel's blackness, hoping to see the headlights of the F.

"You will be helped," he called.

"Huh?"

"I said, you will be helped. You helped another, and so you will be helped. That is one of the ways of our world. Give and you shall be given."

"Okay, pal," I said. "Take care."

The man sat down on the bench, mumbling something to himself.

Eventually, two bright lights appeared through the darkness, and the F train pulled up beside me. I stepped in and stood against the center pole for one more stop, getting out in the LES.

The early morning sun blinded me as I walked up the stairs and headed down Houston. I was pissed when I realized that I didn't have my sunglasses.

"Byron?"

I looked around for who had called my name.

"Byron! Behind you!"

When I turned, Norah was standing there, sipping a piping hot cup of tea.

"What are you doin' *here*?" I asked, surprised.

"What the hell do ya think I'm doing out this early on a Sunday morning? I'm headed to my shift at the hospital. What about you?"

I didn't answer.

"Well, since you're here," she said, "do you wanna walk me to work?"

"Sure," I said.

We started to stroll south toward Gouverneur Hospital.

"Byron, you look like shit. Look at the black around your eyes. Jesus Christ."

"Ma, please."

"Ma please *what*? Did you even sleep yet?"

"Of course."

"If you did sleep, it wasn't for very long."

Norah grabbed her Capri 100s from her purse and lit one up. "So anyway, how are things going in general, huh? How are ya?"

"I can't complain too much," I said. "I met a girl a few months ago."

"You did? Oh, my goodness. Byron, how could you not tell me? What's her name?"

"Cecilia."

"What is she? Italian? Italian girls have good childbearing hips."

"She's Brazilian."

"So what's the deal with her? Do you like her? I mean, *like* her like her?"

"Yeah. She's a good girl. A keeper."

"Oooh. You really *do* like her. A mother can tell these things. When can I meet her, huh?"

"Soon. We're just taking things slow, but I promise you'll meet her."

"I would hope so, Byron Bella," she said with a wink. Taking a drag, she added, "You know, Byron, I want you to be happy and healthy. I don't wanna have to worry about you — worry about getting a phone call in the middle of the night to pick you up at the station."

"You're my mom. If you didn't worry, I would wonder if you cared. But you have to trust me. You raised me right. You remember when it was just us two for a while? Way before Will?"

"I sure do. You were so cute and clever. Endless promise. You know that, Byron? You really could've been almost anything you wanted."

"Ma, I still can be. I'm only twenty-eight. Jesus, you're disheartening sometimes. I just don't know what the hell I wanna be. *Who* I wanna be."

"I hope you figure it all out, sweetie. Just promise me when you do, that you will follow it through to the end."

"What does that mean?"

"Byron, let's be honest here. You can be very indecisive. You second-guess yourself, and I think it hinders you from moving forward and taking care of your business."

"Ma, cut me some slack. Please."

"What about when you kept switching musical instruments in elementary school until you just quit altogether, huh? Same with sports. Or when you kept picking different colleges to apply to? You ended up not applying to *any*."

"Maybe one day that will be different," I said, not fully believing myself.

"Possibly," Norah said, taking a drag from her Capri. "I really hope so, darling. But you saw what happened to your dad and then Willis. It can all be so short. You never know when you're gonna go. That's what makes it all so precious."

"So you want me to live every day like it's my last?" I asked sarcastically.

"Byron, I know you're not gonna live every day like it's your last. Because in reality that's bullshit anyway." She took another drag. "But you have to create your life, or it will be created for you. And trust me, Byron, that's not as much fun. You hear me over there?"

"Yeah, I got you. Just give me some time. I'm workin' on it." I paused. "How do you do it?"

"What?"

"The routine. You wake up every morning, get your tea, and go to the hospital to work."

"That's what grown-ups do, Byron. We have babies and go

to work to pay for them. That's what being an adult is. It's called responsibility."

I said nothing.

"Anyway, what's up with your partner in crime, Mr. Primo?"

"He's alright. Actually, he could probably be better. He seems depressed. But I'm really not sure."

"It's easy to get depressed when you don't do anything productive all day."

"I suppose," I said in agreement.

She stopped in front of the hospital entrance and flicked her cigarette to the ground, crushing it out with a twist of her foot. Looking at me deeply, she gently placed the back of her hand on my scruffy chin.

"Byron," she said, "you know I love you, right?"

"Yeah. Of course."

"Byron, listen to me."

I stared into her eyes. Her face was more wrinkled and her hair was sprinkled with more white than I had realized.

"I love you," she said. "I love you more than anything in this world. It's just me and you again, kiddo. I got you, and you got me."

I nodded and kissed her on the forehead.

She went inside the hospital to take her place in the routine.

31

"How much is it?" Ajani asked. He could see his breath in front of him.

"Three hundred bucks, buckaroo," Primo answered. "And that's me not chargin' you a dime. Just keep the shit outta sight, and don't bring it to school, aight?"

"Who's this?" Ajani asked.

"Franky Golden," Primo answered.

The three sat at the Mound under an overcast sky. A cool gust of wind blew across the East River, and then there was stillness.

"Are there any other options?" Ajani asked.

"Look, kid," replied Franky, "dis is a twenty-two Magnum. It's small and priced to sell. Trust me. Dis little sucker is all you'll ever need." He gripped the gun by its cherry-stained wood grain handle. "It's compact, but the stainless steel gives it a decent weight. Feel."

Ajani took the mini revolver and felt the smooth, cold metal against his palm. "The barrel reminds me of those old Westerns on late-night TV." Ajani aimed the gun in front of him and innocently pointed it in Primo's direction.

"Yo! Don't point that shit at me, aight?" Primo's nose was running uncontrollably, his pupils were like pin tips, and when he sniffled, he wiped his nose with the sleeve of his hoodie.

"Sorry," Ajani said, embarrassed.

"You like the twenty-two, right? I can tell," said Golden. "Gimme three hundred and we're good."

"I'm down," Ajani said.

There was a faint roar in the sky. The boy looked up and spotted a plane descending through the gang of charcoal-colored clouds that hung drearily overhead.

"Dose 747s fly up and down all day and night, right?" Franky asked. "They don't quit."

"Actually," the boy explained in a muted voice, "that's not a 747. It's an Airbus, like the one that crash-landed in the river a while back."

"You mean, the Miracle on the Hudson?" Primo asked.

"Yeah." Ajani pointed up at the descending plane. "That one right there is about to land in Newark." He looked at the gun. "What about bullets for this shit?"

"Here, you can have dese on the house," Franky said, handing the boy a few bullets. "Just make sure if you ever use dose, you get in close and don't miss. Dis piece ain't known for its accuracy."

"Why do you need this shit, anyway?" Primo asked. "Is someone botherin' ya?"

"Nah. I just want it as insurance, ya know? In case shit happens."

"Yeah, well I heard you had a bit of an incident by your fat friend's crib the other day," Golden said.

"How *you* know that?" Ajani asked.

"Never mind how he knows," Primo said. "You ever fire a piece before?"

"Yeah," Ajani answered with his chest puffed out. "My friend, Chris Parker, his pops took us upstate a few times and let us fire some rounds off his hunting rifle. The shit hurt my shoulder. But I never shot one like this." The boy gently stroked the revolver. "Here," he said as he handed Golden some beat-up bills.

"Byron doesn't need to know about this, aight?" said Primo. "This is our little secret. I'm just tryin' to help ya out, bro."

"Yeah," said Ajani. "I don't really need him knowing about this, either."

"I mean, we all love B here, but he's kind of a square sometimes," Primo added.

The boy nodded in agreement while he stuffed the .22 and the three bullets in his school bag alongside his English and history books.

"Yo, Franky," Primo said, scratching his neck. "I'm gonna need a piece soon, too."

"No prob. I got a nine-milli semi wit your name on it. Ya need to check it out ASAP. Practically brand-new."

"You always seem to got what I need, Franky."

"Hey, whateva a person *needs* is exactly what I can make a buck on. Ya know what I'm sayin', Primo?"

"For real," Primo said, starting to shiver. "I think it's time to get outta here already."

"Yeah," Golden said, "I'm freezin' my goddamn plums off!"

As the three wedged themselves out through the fence that bordered the park, Ajani looked up in the sky one last time. Nothing to see except overcast.

32

It was a gloomy moonless night. No stars either. I was blasting Sharon Jones from my iPhone as I approached the front steps of my building.

> *This land is your land.*
> *This land is my land.*
> *From California,*
> *Well, to the New York island.*

As I pulled out my key and opened the old wooden door, I felt somebody jab me in the lower back. I struggled at first, but then someone else grabbed my right shoulder and pushed me forward.

As the three of us were crammed in the vestibule between two red doors, I peeked behind me and saw a couple of kids as young as fifteen.

The tall black kid pulled out one of my ear buds. "What's goin' on, B?" he asked.

"Do I know you?" I turned off the music.

"We're acquaintances with your boys Ajani and Pedro and Chris Parker," the black kid replied.

"I don't even know that pudgeball Pedro or Chris Parker. How do you know Ajani?"

"Open the other door and we'll tell ya inside, motherfucker," the white kid said. He was wearing a cubic zirconia in his ear and a Dodgers cap low on his brow.

"Alright, but watch your attitude, kid. You might get a slap."

"You feel this fuckin' ratchet in your ribs, motherfucker? Just open the fuckin' door like we been sayin'," the white kid snapped, more vexed than before.

I did as they ordered and unlocked the second entry door.

"Your boy Ajani's been playin' people, homie," said the black kid. "Sellin' stepped-on bullshit. He ripped me off one time too many. Ya know what I'm sayin'? But all that is stoppin' right now. *I* get the last laugh!"

"Yo, Al, they ripped me off, too," said the white kid. He whispered creepily in my ear, "I hate those fuckin' fuckwads."

"Don't be usin' my name, nigga!" Al scolded his partner, whose face turned beet red. "Push the button, prick," Al said to me.

When the elevator door opened, they shoved me inside and we headed vertical.

"What *I* wanna know," I said, "is why the hell are ya botherin' *me* about this shit?"

"Because," Al said, "we know that you're his supplier, homie. That's why."

I laughed, much to their dismay. "Are you kiddin' me? I don't fuck with that garbage. I hate coke. Your info is way off, you brats."

"Bullshit, nigga!" Al yelled.

"Don't lie to us, B," the white boy said. "We know you two are from the same hood. We still see him with you hangin' around the block. Playin' ball."

"Yeah," Al said. "We know you's lyin'! No more fuckin' lies!"

As we got off the elevator, all I could think about was Cecilia—right there in my apartment, getting ready for our dinner reservation in Little Italy. We were hoping to work on our relationship. Instead this.

"I'm tellin' ya, I don't have shit. Especially no blow," I said, sitting on my living room couch.

By now, Cecilia was sitting nervously next to me.

"We'll see what you got." Al pointed to Cecilia's purse, which was resting on her lap. "Like that bag right there for starters. What's that, huh? Prada? Huh?"

"Marc Jacobs," she answered quietly.

"Yeah, I could tell it was that *real* shit," Al said. "Just stay frozen on that couch. And don't move a fuckin' muscle, or I swear you'll get blasted."

The two started to ransack my living room, the whole time insisting that I had somehow wronged them, and I'd better rectify the situation—or else. Al soon made his way to my bedroom.

I could have taken a chance by trying to attack the white boy, waiting for him to let down his guard, but I knew that could be bad. What if Cecilia got hurt? Hell, if *anyone* were to get seriously roughed up, it would be very bad for me. I didn't need men in blue snooping around my crib. So it was worth giving up anything I had in the apartment and letting the little creeps take what they wanted.

Cecilia softly rested her palm on mine. But the look in her eyes—something startled me. Frightened me.

Armed with a Taser in her other palm, she bellowed from deep within, "Fuck you, motherfucker!"

The white kid tried to scramble away, but it was no use. Cecilia jumped up and zapped the shit out of him until he was on the floor, wriggling spastically. His gun involuntarily fell from his hand, so I snatched it.

"I got it! I got!" Al cheered triumphantly, walking back into the living room with stacks of cash in each hand. "What the fuck was all that noise, though, my nigg—?" Shocked, he saw his boy struggling mightily on the floor and me aiming a piece at his sternum.

"Drop the money *now*," Cecilia demanded.

"Then get the fuck outta here," I added. "And take your lover boy with you. Fuckin' amateurs. Two bitch-ass rookies. That's all you are."

Al dropped the stacks on the couch, grabbed his fried friend, and scurried out the door.

Cecilia began to cry as I held her tightly.

33

"Yeah?" Chilly said as he answered the door for the UPS guy.

"Hi, sir," the deliveryman said. "You got a package. Just need a signature."

"Really? I wasn't expecting."

"No," the man said, holding out a cardboard box, "I definitely have a package with your name on it, sir."

Chilly squinted his eyes to get a better look at the lanky man in front of him, from his toes all the way up to his brown cap.

"You ain't no UPS guy."

"Of course, I am, sir. What would make you say that?"

"You ain't no UPS guy," Chilly repeated. "UPS guys ain't wearin' white Nike Dunks to work. Especially not in the dead of winter. You know what I think? I think you're full of shit."

In all brown, except for his sneakers, the skinny man looked fleetingly to his right at his partner who was just out of Chilly's view. Then he charged forward with all his might, growling as he grabbed Chilly by the collar, and shoved him back into the apartment. His partner scurried in to help take Chilly down.

Once inside, Sal shut the front door and locked it, as Slim threw Chilly to the couch. Pulling out a stainless steel Beretta that was tucked in his jeans, Sal said, "Gimme your cell phone!"

Chilly reached over to his marble coffee table, which was littered with dried pot shake, and handed Slim the phone without ever taking his eyes off Sal. A special on the Seven Seas was quietly playing on the flat screen in the corner.

"What the fuck is this all about?" said Chilly. "Who sent you here? Who do you represent?"

Sal walked over to the landline phone that was sitting on a desk and violently ripped the cord out of the wall. "You don't worry who I represent. You just need to worry about what I say right now. If you cooperate, we can all walk away from this uninjured. And by we, I mean *you*."

"What the hell do you want *me* to do?" Chilly moved his eyes from Sal to Slim, who stood looming over him.

"What I want you to do," Sal said, "is give up those coins you found at the bottom of the fuckin' sea. And any other shit you think we should take," he added through a Cheshire Cat–like grin.

"Someone sold me out, huh?" Chilly said. "Who was it? How much did they pay you? Shit, I bet you didn't even get paid yet, did ya? I bet I can offer more. But I wanna know who sent you and this brainless shmohawk over here."

Slim was about to curse Chilly out when Sal stifled him by holding up his hand. "We know who you are, Chilly. And you don't know shit about us. Nothin'!" Sal yelled. "And that's how it's gonna stay. Got me? Just get your old ass up and make your way to where the coins are."

While Sal was barking orders, Slim was eyeing all the foreign-looking weapons hanging on the walls. The paintings of lion packs, huge angry elephants, and menacing apes stared down at him from all angles. His confidence began to deflate more and more with each passing second.

Noticing his weak-minded brother's doubtful expression, Sal tried to move things along. "Now!" he shouted at Chilly. "Get up and let's go!"

Chilly was slow to get up. He looked at one of the four-foot by four-foot paintings on the wall and then over at Slim. "Hey, man in brown," he said. "With the white Nikes. You like my lions? My elephants? My apes? All eyes on you right now, buddy. And I can tell you—they don't look too pleased." Chilly gave a sinister wink.

Slim looked more closely at the walls. African war clubs, Samurai swords, and three-pronged Aboriginal spears, all used for stabbing and bludgeoning, hung proudly beside dozens of pairs of wild eyes.

Watching as Slim took in all of his surroundings, Chilly laughed out loud at the UPS impostor, making him all the more uncomfortable.

"Old man!" Sal yelled, desperately trying to keep control of the situation. Shoving the Beretta a few inches from Chilly's head, he said, "Coins! Now!"

"Follow me."

Chilly led the way down the stairs to the basement. Slim followed closely while Sal trailed behind. The vintage radio box in the basement was tuned to the oldies station as usual. Chilly kneeled down in front of a steel safe against the wall and started to twist the combination knob.

"You guys like oldies?" he asked. "*I* sure do. Doesn't matter who. The Righteous Brothers. Elvis. The Big Bopper. The Beach Boys—*early* Beach Boys, that is. They're all wonderful. What about you?"

"Nah, I don't listen to that shit," Sal said, caught off guard by the question. "Some of that shit gives me the creeps."

"Not even Buddy Holly?" Chilly asked.

"Nope," Sal said. "I think I saw his movie once, though."

"Nah," said Slim. "He died in a plane crash way back in the day. That was an *actor* in the movie. Gary Busey, I think."

"I know it was an actor, you fuckin' idiot!" yelled Sal. "And I don't give two shits about crazy-ass Gary Busey right now!"

"This guy is a real mook, huh?" said Chilly.

"No more chitchat from you, guy," said Sal. "Just finish with the combo already, alright? We need to get the fuck outta here."

Chilly grabbed the cross-shaped handle and spun it until there was a cracking noise. As he pulled on the cold metal handle, the heavy door creaked open. The safe was completely dark inside.

"Now get me the coins," Sal ordered.

"What coins?" Chilly asked.

"The fuckin' coins from the goddamn yacht," answered Sal. "Don't play coy with me, old man. We ain't got the time for that."

Chilly reached into the safe as Slim stood right behind him with his arms crossed. Sal was only a few steps away. Chilly turned around with a burgundy velour pouch full of coins in his hand. "This is what you want, right?"

Sal nodded.

Chilly tossed the pouch up in Sal's direction and reached back into his safe. With the ferocity of a grizzly bear, he roared out and lunged backwards, swinging at Slim's long exposed neck.

The tiger shark teeth of Chilly's Fijian *leiomano* blade lacerated both of Slim's forearms just as he put them up to block his neck from getting slit.

Slim backed up in horror, watching his blood spurt out and stain the light green carpet beneath him.

Sal desperately reached for the Beretta he had already tucked back in his jeans, but Chilly wasted no time attacking him with the thin samurai *tanto* he was hiding behind his left forearm. As the small sword ripped through Sal's wool coat, blood started to pour. Chilly's eyes cried victory as he wound up, ready to strike Sal with a deathblow.

Slim violently wrapped an arm around Chilly's neck just in time to stop the advance on his brother. Chilly dropped the Japanese dagger to rip the velour pouch from Sal's hand, sending coins flying everywhere.

Slim squeezed tighter and pulled Chilly backwards until they both fell to the floor. Chilly dropped the *leiomano* in his right hand while trying to break his fall. He attempted to scream at the top of his lungs, but it came out more like a gurgling sound. This scared the shit out of Slim, who was lying underneath, still with a deep chokehold.

Standing over the two men, Sal fired off three shots into Chilly's torso. One shot pierced through his side and lodged in Slim's thigh.

The second and third hit dead center. Slim didn't let go of Chilly's neck until the pulsating stopped. Then he pushed the body off him and slowly got to his feet.

"Look at me!" Slim shouted. "I'm bleedin' all over! What the fuck did you shoot me for?!"

"You got shot 'cause you're a moron! That's why! You weren't payin' fuckin' attention! That's what happens when you don't pay attention. He slashed my fuckin' gut." Sal was ranting. "How do you think *I* feel? Thank god my coat took most of it… You ain't gonna die, are ya? You ain't feelin' dizzy?"

"I'm pretty banged up, Sal. My arms are fucked. We gotta go to an emergency room."

"First, pick up all the coins. They're all over the fuckin' floor." Sal looked at the ancient Lydian coins scattered around the lifeless body below him. "This asshole had to fight back."

While Slim picked up the loose coins, Sal peered in the safe.

"Anythin' else worth takin'?" Slim asked.

"Nah. Plus, this already got way outta hand. We're leavin' with what we came for, and that's good for now. Someone could've heard the shots."

"Fine." Slim scooped up two more coins and shoved them in his pocket. "I think I got 'em all."

"Good," Sal said. "Now let's get the hell outta here."

34

DON'T YOU THINK IT'S TIME
WE THOUGHT ABOUT THE FUTURE?
WHETHER OUR CHILDREN
THEY GONNA BE WINNERS OR LOSERS?

—KRS-ONE
"THE MIND"

I'M SICK OF WORRYING. THE PARANOIA. THE
DRUGS. THE MONEY. THE TREPIDATION OF GETTING
CAUGHT BY THE COPS. OR WORSE—STUCK UP
AGAIN BY SOME SECOND-RATE CHILD CROOKS. THE
CONSTANT UNCERTAINTY OF MY WHOLE DAMN LIFE
IS DRAINING ME.

SOME TIME HAS PASSED BY SINCE AJANI'S
PROBLEMS SPILLED ON TO ME, THICK AND DARK
AS TAR. HE APOLOGIZED TO ME AND I ACCEPTED
WITHOUT HESITATION. WHAT CAN I SAY? I LOVE
THE LIL' FUCKER. I MADE HIM APOLOGIZE TO
CECILIA FOR DRAGGING HER INTO HIS MESS.
I PROBABLY SHOULD HAVE AS WELL. I HAVE
SERIOUS DOUBTS THAT SHE WILL STICK AROUND A
DEGENERATE LIKE YOURS TRULY.

WILL THERE BE A DAY FOR ME WHEN I SAY
ENOUGH IS ENOUGH ALREADY? MAKE CHANGES?
MOVE FORWARD? NOT SURE YET. I'M A MAJOR
PROCRASTINATOR.

I sipped my coffee in Everyman Espresso, reflecting.

After those two pieces of shit had left my apartment a couple of weeks back, Cecilia and I cleaned up, and then headed over to her place to hide out for a bit. I found myself fighting off strong feelings of self-pity and anger. I wanted to quit the game forever. But the burdening truth was becoming obvious—I had to get more product and make some cash fast. New York City demanded it. Even with the paranoia that was flowing through my veins, the show must go on.

No one knew who my connect was. Not Primo. No one. And it wasn't more than a few days before I was at our normal meeting spot—a quiet cobble-stoned street right near the Holland Tunnel. As usual, she had pulled up in front of me in her green Volkswagen Passat with California plates. I told her what had happened. She grabbed a worn canvas bag from the trunk, handed it to me, and gave me a warm embrace. She also told me that everything would work out and to keep my chakras clear. I told her I would try. Since then, I've just been taking it day by day.

I finished my coffee, stuffed my journal in my back pocket, and walked to Chilly's brownstone down the block to collect a small debt. Only a light dusting of snow covered the pavement, but the forecast called for heavier storms.

I rang the doorbell twice. No one answered. Chilly always answered on the first ring. He would dash to the door with joint in hand, ready to go. I twisted the front doorknob to see if it was locked. It wasn't. I poked my head through.

"Hey, yo, Chilly!" I shouted. "Hey, Chilly, where you at?"

There was no response. In the living room, the TV was on the Nature Channel, as always. There was a special on snakes. Chilly hated snakes. Just like Indiana Jones.

I shouted for him again, but still there was no reply. I knew that he could be downstairs, working away—probably looking up new information about one of his treasures while cleaning and polishing another. As I walked over to the staircase that led down to the basement, I saw that the light was on and could hear the Beach

Boys' "Good Vibrations" playing on Chilly's favorite oldies station.

"Chilly?" I called.

There was no answer.

I headed down the steps, assuming he was there. Was he hiding from me? Chilly adored messing around with me, trying to play kindergarten pranks like a five-year-old high on cola.

If this was a game of hide-and-seek, it was ill-conceived. Chilly was on the floor, on his back, with his arms spread. I looked at his safe. It was wide open. All I could see inside were a few antique knives sitting on a stack of papers.

I put two fingers to his bruised neck. No pulse. Then I saw bullet wounds. Now what? Most people would have called the police. Like immediately. But my fear and loathing of them prevented me. Shit, those cynical detective bastards would think I was involved. I swallowed, trying to push down the lump in my throat. It was no use.

The samurai dagger lying next to Chilly's carcass had blood along the edge. So did the serrated tiger shark teeth on the *leiomano* that was resting on the other side of the body. There was a battle in here. The crazy bastard didn't cave easily. From the stories he told me, I would've expected nothing less.

Suddenly, I noticed his left hand. It wasn't open like his right. It was clenched up tightly in a fist. I pulled the hand open, and there in the center of his dead white palm was a coin.

I recognized it instantly. I would have to be an idiot not to. It was identical to the ones he had shown Primo and me on the *Angelfish*. As I was still on my knees, I saw the burgundy pouch that once held all the coins from Chilly's excursion. The velour had been ripped to shreds.

Scared shitless, I grabbed the coin and bolted up the stairs.

Before leaving the building, I glanced around the living room on my way out, looking for missing stuff. I mean, this guy had shit worth money on every surface. It seemed that nothing had been touched aside from the Lydian coins, although I was far from certain. I felt sick to my stomach and needed to get the hell out of there.

35

"Yeah?"

"It's me," said the voice on the phone.

"Where the fuck you been? I've been tryin' to call you for, like, twelve hours. What the fuck?"

Primo was impatient and ready to pounce on any answer Sal gave.

"We had a major problem."

"What do you mean?"

"What I mean is, you didn't tell me that the fish I went to hook was a goddamn shark."

"Is everything good?"

"No, it's not good. Sharks bite! They bite hard!"

"Just come by my spot, aight? We'll talk."

"Yeah. I'll be there real fuckin' soon. Three minutes, tops."

Primo chopped up lines of coke on a mirror that was resting on his lap. He grabbed a rolled-up twenty that was encrusted with residue at the ends and snorted two large ones.

A car horn honked. Primo got up and walked down the three flights of stairs. His 9mm was tucked behind him at his waist. There, standing in the falling snow, were the Balducci brothers. Sal was casually sitting on the hood of his black Lincoln Town Car. Slim was standing next to him with bandages on his arms, one in a sling.

"What happened to you?" Primo asked.

"Your boy fuckin' slashed me with somethin' that had fuckin' shark teeth. That's what fuckin' happened."

"Slim, be easy," said Sal, while still looking at Primo. "Your man was not an easy mark, Primo. You didn't warn us that he could be a problem. That's gonna definitely cost ya extra." Sal chewed his toothpick slowly and deliberately.

"That's bullshit. We made a deal. We said—"

Sal interrupted, "Now I say another two grand. I say that you set us up for a problem instead of doin' your homework."

"We had to go to a hospital in Jersey and tell 'em we got mugged," said Slim. "It was fuckin' humiliatin'. The bill for that alone was more than a grand. I told my brother we should just split the coins ourselves."

"Yo, Sal. Why are you lettin' him speak? I thought he's supposed to just stand next to you, lookin' stupid and ugly as ever."

"Everyone just take it easy," said Sal. "An extra thousand, we got a deal?"

"No," Primo answered.

"I figured you might feel that way," Sal said. "That's why we kept a few coins for our troubles."

He nodded to his flustered partner, who reached into the glove compartment, pulled out a clear Ziploc, and begrudgingly handed it over.

"This is unbelievable," Primo said, frowning at the bag of Lydian coins. "You think you're gonna come in front of *my* building, to *my* home, and shake *me* down? Like I'm some custy? We already had a deal in place." He pulled out his piece, looking sweaty and possessed. His eyes were bulging. "A fuckin' deal! You ain't seein' another cent from me! Not one more motherfuckin' cent! Now get the hell outta here, Sal, before I blow off your pinky toe! And take your mongoloid of a brother with ya!"

The Balducci brothers backed up cautiously and got into the

Town Car. Just before Sal pulled away, he rolled down his tinted side window and said, "Better keep that gun by your pillow, Primo. You're gonna need it real soon."

Primo kept his 9mm aimed straight ahead.

As the car peeled away, spraying icy slush behind it, Primo tried to calm himself. He put the safety back on his gun and headed toward the front entrance of his building with the Ziploc stashed in his coat pocket. Just then his Droid rang. It was an unfamiliar number.

36

"Hello?"

"Yo, Primo, it's B."

"What's good, man? What number are ya callin' me from?"

"Never mind that. I got a fuckin' problem, my dude." I was trying not to sound scared. "Yo, man, you gotta meet me right now."

"I just got home. I was about to go upstairs and shower. Can we link in an hour?"

"Nah, Primo. You gotta meet me right now. I'm in the East Village. I'll meet you by 7th and C."

"Yeah, but I gotta—"

"Fuck that shit! Meet me right now!" I hung up the phone.

A bag of nerves. Each minute that passed brought more visions of Chilly lying there dead as doornails. Stiff as a board. It was horrible.

When I got to the meeting spot, Primo was already there, standing with his hands in his pockets.

"What's up, homie?" he asked, giving me daps.

"Let's go over to the Mound. I'm supposed to meet Ajani over there soon. Besides, it's private. I gotta tell ya what I just saw. I need some fuckin' fresh air. I feel fuckin' sick."

"Aight. What was so urgent, though?"

"It's my boy Chilly." It was hard for me to explain at first. I mean, where would I begin?

"The treasure hunter? How's he doin'?"

"Not fuckin' good."

"Why?"

"He's dead. I was in his house just now. He's gone."

Primo looked at me with his eyebrows raised. "Holy shit, yo. How? I mean, what happened?"

"I went over to his house, ya know?"

"Yeah."

"His door was unlocked, so when he didn't answer, I went in. He was in the basement. He was fuckin' strangled and shot up. I never seen anythin' like it."

Primo didn't respond.

"I checked to see if he was alive, but he wasn't."

"So what did you do?"

"What the fuck *could* I do? I ran up the block and called you from a payphone."

"Did you touch anythin'? I mean, your prints?"

I held up my hands, showing Primo my gloves.

"Good," he said. "Maybe they were crackheads in a rush. You know how those crillheads rob shit. They'll take anythin'. A cup full of pennies. Old appliances. Whatever."

"It was weird, though."

"Why?"

"Because nothin' was really taken. I mean, there was stuff to take all over the place. They didn't take *shit*. Just some coins."

"That's what I'm tellin' ya. Crackheads will come in just for some fistfuls of coins. They're nuts."

"Not *any* coins," I said. "The same ones he showed us when we hung with him on the *Angelfish*."

"Really? That's fuckin' crazy. Maybe he had some enemies, ya know? He probably had his share."

"Why do you say that?"

"Most rich guys do. Who knows who he's pissed off, or who wanted to set him up and why? The sin of mankind."

I looked over at Primo as we walked through the freshly laid flakes.

"What the hell did you do?" I asked.

"What are you talkin' about?" Primo was instantly defensive. His voice was sharp.

"You know exactly what I'm fuckin' talkin' about."

"No," he said. "I really don't have a clue. Why don't you fill me in?"

"You knew about the coins. Chilly told us on his boat. And you knew where he lived, 'cause you've been there with me. You *fucked* me, Primo! And Chilly's dead now!"

"You knew about those coins, too! Maybe *you* did it, for all we—"

"Don't, Primo! Just don't. We both know it wasn't me. What the fuck happened? Just tell me why?"

"Yo, B, back the hell off, you crazy fuck!" He leaned in, face-to-face. "I'm tellin' ya I didn't take *nothin'* from Chilly! I don't wanna talk about that shit no more!"

There was an uneasy silence as we crossed over the highway on the overpass and headed down the ramp to East River Park.

When we reached the tall bushes that hid the Mound at the end of the promenade and slid through the hole in the fence, Ajani wasn't there.

"Byron, I've got somethin' to show ya," Primo said, pulling out a Ziploc bag and pouring a couple of coins into his hand.

"You *did* kill Chilly!"

"No, I didn't!"

"Who did, Primo, huh?"

"Fuckin' cocaine… and all those goddamn pills." His jaw clenched and his eyes bulged. "Sometimes I don't know if I'm goin' north or south."

"What the fuck does that have to do with Chilly?"

"Look," Primo said, rubbing his forehead, "I owe Javier some cash. A bunch. He said if I didn't pay him soon, he would send the hyenas after me, B. Chilly was supposed to just give these guys the goods, and it all would've worked out."

"And were you gonna pay off Javier and keep the extra coins for yourself?"

He didn't answer.

How could Primo let his life get to such a point of disarray? Who was this person in front of me? I thought we were cut from the same cloth. I thought we've been living by some sort of unwritten code—we sell, we don't rob.

It was getting darker, and the snow was coming down with more force.

"Why don't we split the coins up?" he said. "You take some, and I'll take the rest."

"No."

"No?"

"No," I repeated. "I can't. You know what, Primo? You need to get outta here right fuckin' now. Lay low. Don't tell anyone about the coins. We'll get in touch in a few days, and then I'm takin' you to a rehab. You need fuckin' help. It stops here."

Primo's face turned beet red with anger. "You think you're better than me? Is that it, B? I think you would've done the same thing if you had to. I taught you what you fuckin' know! Remember that shit!"

"You're outta control, Primo."

"Don't act so innocent. You love to get high as much as me. You know how I know? 'Cause we were sittin' right next to each other."

"Yeah, but Primo, we gotta grow up, man. Bein' wasted all the time—I don't wanna live like that forever. Do you? Don't you ever wanna just be sober? Comfortable in your own skin? Comfortable with your own self?"

"You live in a dream world," Primo sneered, rubbing his face vigorously. "You got nothin' goin' on except the same bullshit as me. So don't put yourself on some fuckin' pedestal, B!"

"Primo, are you nuts? I might be doin' nothin' with my life, but I'm not about to take someone else's. Do you realize what just happened? I don't even think you get it!"

"I told you! It wasn't supposed to go down that way! I just wanted the fuckin' coins, but your boy got crazy, aight? He spazzed out and got himself killed." Putting an arm around me, he said, "I know you liked the guy, B, but to hell with it. *We're* still here, ain't we? Let's just agree that it wasn't the best move and leave it at that. Leave it in the past."

Who was this person with his arm locked tightly on my shoulder? I wanted Primo back—the Primo who taught me how to smoke, how to get girls, how to live.

"You need help," was all that came out of my mouth.

I felt disturbingly alone with my best friend at the edge of the river.

"I'm outta here, man," I said. "I'm gonna find Ajani. Do what I told you, Primo, and lay low."

As I walked back to the fence, I heard a gun cock. Spinning around, I saw Primo pointing a 9mm right at me.

"When the hell did you get that?" I asked.

"B, I did what I did, aight? No turning back now. And if you won't back me up and split these coins... well, I don't think I can trust you anymore. In fact, this could work out even better. I'll just keep *all* the extra coins, like I was gonna in the first place. I could use the extra cash."

"Just give me the ratchet," I begged.

Primo's expression turned from anger to desperation. In his wet, bloodshot eyes, I finally saw my kindred spirit again. My amigo. He was drowning in a lake of sorrow, and I had no life preserver to throw him.

Behind me, I heard rustling by the hole in the fence.

Two shots rang out!

Primo dropped the 9mm, put both of his hands on his bloody gut, and stumbled to the snowy ground.

I dropped as well, pressing my hand against my left shoulder, trying to stop the bleeding. With every ounce of strength I had, I turned to look behind me. Ajani was standing there with his mouth open and a small smoking gun at his side.

"You have to get outta here now," I said. "You got me? Did you get your prints on that thing?"

Ajani showed me the gloves I had given him.

"Good. Now throw that shit in the river. The gloves too. Do it!"

Ajani hurled the gun into the icy water. Followed by the gloves.

I reached into my coat pocket and gave him the gold coin that I had pried from Chilly's cold dead hand.

"Take care of this for me, too," I said, handing the boy my journal from my back pocket. "Keep it safe for me."

"I will."

"Hey," I said in pain. "Where were you?"

"I stayed after school to talk to Janet. I guess we lost track of time."

"That's my boy," I said with a grin.

"I saw Primo yellin' through the fence when I got here. He was pointin' that gun at you and, I mean, I had to do somethin', right?"

My vision was starting to blur, and my mouth was dry, but I was able to mutter, "You did what you had to, lil' man. Now get lost."

Ajani paused by Primo for a second and slid back through the hole in the fence that separated the Mound from the rest of the promenade.

I was hunched over a large flat stone, trying to stay conscious. Primo was lying in blood red snow in front of me. Mumbling. Dying. I heard sirens. I saw black.

37

COURAGE IS RESISTANCE TO FEAR, MASTERY OF
FEAR —NOT ABSENCE OF FEAR.

—MARK TWAIN
PUDD'NHEAD WILSON'S CALENDAR

WHERE DID IT ALL GO SO WRONG, PRIMO?
HATING YOURSELF —WHAT YOU HAD BECOME.
HOPELESS FOR HUMANITY. FRIGHTFUL OF THE
FUTURE. LOOK WHERE IT GOT YOU. TRAPPED ON
DRUGS. IMPRISONED BY NEGATIVITY. LOCKED UP
IN A PINE BOX? NOT ME. I PREFER TO GO LIKE
WILLIS. BURN ME UP FAST, AND SET MY ASHES
FREE.

SPEAKING OF FREE, CECILIA LEFT FOR PARIS
WEEKS AGO. LOVE LETTERS MAYBE, BUT I WON'T
BE GOING FOR A VISIT ANYTIME SOON, WILL I?

MY PUBLIC DEFENDER MAY HAVE GOT ME OFF
ON SELF-DEFENSE, BUT THANKS TO MAYOR MIKE
THE STOLEN .22 THAT THEY FOUND AT THE BOTTOM
OF THE EAST RIVER CAME WITH A MANDATORY.

SO HERE I AM. HERE I AM WITH A PEN AND
PAPER AGAIN. STAYING OUT OF THE WAY FOR
THIRTY-TWO MORE MONTHS. THAT'S CERTAINLY

PLENTY OF TIME TO THINK. TO WRITE. TO WRITE OFTEN. FOR ME AND THE ONES I CARE FOR WITH ABSOLUTELY NO SHAME. RESISTING MY FEARS! LUCKILY FOR ME, PENNY'S NEW PROJECT, "THE WILLOW: SHORT STORIES OF REVELATION," HAD ROOM FOR A NEWCOMER.

BELIEVE ME, I KNOW IT MUST SOUND BIZARRE FROM INSIDE THIS CAGE, BUT IT'S LIKE I FEEL— UNSTOPPABLE. LIKE, EVEN THOUGH THE SHIT HIT THE FAN, STILL, THERE IS AN ETERNAL FLAME DEEP DOWN THAT GLOWS WITH HOPE AND ANTICIPATION.

JUST AS SPRING SEEDLINGS STRETCH FROM CRACKS IN CITY SIDEWALKS, WE ALL HAVE THE CHANCE TO START OVER AFTER A RUTHLESS WINTER. TO RIGHT WRONGS. TO BE REBORN. TO CREATE SOMETHING SPECIAL, SOMETIMES FROM HARDLY ANYTHING AT ALL.

INSIDE THESE PRISON WALLS MAY BE MY CURSE, BUT THE LIFE AND LOVED ONES THAT AWAIT ME ON THE OUTSIDE—THAT MUST SURELY BE THE BLESSING. THE YIN AND THE YANG, I SUPPOSE.

38

When the bell rang, children broke out of their school-induced malaise with glee. Groups formed around the classroom as the kids put their coats on. They were discussing what games they would play or what food they would munch on from the bodega, now that the school day had passed.

Not Ajani. He was his normal even-keeled self. The boy got his bag together, put on his rain jacket, walked out the main entrance, and gave a nod to a couple of friends who waved to him. Today he didn't stop to talk. He just kept walking east.

It was a drizzly March day. The strong wind cut through Ajani's small frame. But that didn't bother the boy. It was refreshing. The seasons were in the midst of changing. Life was getting ready to bloom again. A new start.

Ajani got out of the train in downtown Brooklyn and walked a few blocks to the laundromat with orchids flourishing in the front window.

Chang was waiting out on the stoop, keeping dry under his awning. His rose-red silk suit with gold *shou* symbols and matching slippers exuded comfort.

"C'mon, lil' man. You're gonna catch the sniffles," he said, leading the boy into the laundromat.

Ajani walked over to Lu Chu, who was taking care of some bills in the back office. She gave him a squeeze. Apprehensive at first, the boy returned the hug. Then he looked over at Chang, who was waiting by the door that led to the basement.

"C'mon." Chang opened the door and extended his arm. "After you, lil' man."

When they were downstairs, Chang took off his slippers and walked over to the tattered punching bag, which was bigger than the boy. Ajani stood and watched as Chang punched the black bag with synchronized yells.

Left jab. Right hook. Right knee. Left head kick.

Chang extended his hand again, this time pointing to the bag.

Ajani lined up in front, spread his legs into horse stance, and performed a similar combination of rapid punches and kicks. His form was disciplined. At the end, he looked at his elder and bowed. The two slapped hands.

Chang slipped into the bathroom, and there was a click. He walked over to the hidden door in the wall that had just popped out, went to black box number 23, and opened the double locks.

Ajani walked up to the open box and saw a new velour pouch filled with ancient Lydian coins. Next to that was a stack of hundreds obtained by selling a couple of the coins to another one of Chang's safe deposit clients. Ajani pulled out two crisp Benjamins. Chang always let the boy take out what he wanted. After all, the box was his. However, the *sifu* carefully watched Ajani to let the boy know he was under close surveillance.

"I think I can sell two more coins tomorrow," Chang said.

"But don't forget—"

"Byron's share. Of course, lil' man."

Ajani seemed somber and slightly distant.

"What is it?" Chang asked. "B again, I presume?"

The boy nodded as he folded his arms.

"I told you before, and all I can do is reiterate. You feel guilty. Wondering why you're here and he's there? But, Ajani, this is how he chose to handle things—to protect you." Chang shut the safe. "And that's the way it is, son. So do him a favor and make him proud in the meantime. I know you will."

Chang then closed up shop and led the boy to the front door of the laundromat. The two slapped hands once again under the awning, and Ajani headed off into the April shower.

After getting off the train back to the Lower East Side, the boy walked over the expressway to the Mound and slipped through the fence. At long last, the clouds cleared and the rain receded. The sky above was a rich array of colors, yellow to magenta. Ajani wiped some water off one of the flat stones next to Janet, who had been patiently waiting for him. He sat down and took off his hood. The two focused on a 747 climbing upward. It was headed somewhere.